Finding Your Place on the Team

Exploring the Sacral Chakra

Created by Yvette Farkas

Illustrated by Jana Rothwell

Finding Your Place on the Team: Exploring the Sacral Chakra (Book 3)
© 2024 by Yvette Farkas

Cover Illustration and Interior Design:
Jana Rothwell

Editing:
Poh Lin Cheng
Sherri Mellamed
Bella Jasper

ISBN:
Finding Your Place on the Team: Exploring the Sacral Chakra (Print book)
978-1-7382155-1-5
Finding Your Place on the Team: Exploring the Sacral Chakra (E-book)
978-1-7382155-2-2
Finding Your Place on the Team: Exploring the Sacral Chakra (Audiobook)
978-1-7382155-3-9

Published by:
Singing Soul Books
Website www.singingsoulbooks.com
Email info@singingsoulbooks.com

Disclaimer:
The techniques and tools presented in this book are intended for personal development and growth. While every effort has been made to ensure the accuracy and effectiveness of the information provided, the author and publisher assume no responsibility for any consequences resulting from the application of the methods described herein. Readers are advised to use their discretion and take personal responsibility for implementing these techniques. Personal development is a subjective journey, and individual results may vary based on personal circumstances, commitment, and application.

It is important to consult with relevant professionals or experts, where appropriate, before applying any of the suggestions in these books, especially if you have underlying health conditions or concerns. The author and publisher disclaim any liability, loss, or risk incurred directly or indirectly as a result of the use and application of the information presented in this book. Furthermore, readers are encouraged to approach personal development with an open mind and consider seeking additional resources, guidance, or support to complement the tools presented in this book. The author does not endorse any specific methodologies or approaches as the sole solution for everyone.

By reading this book, you acknowledge and agree that you are fully responsible for your own choices, actions, and outcomes. The author and publisher shall not be held liable for any damages, losses, or adverse consequences arising directly or indirectly from the information provided in this book.

Your personal development journey is uniquely yours, and this book serves as a guide rather than a definitive prescription. Embrace it with an open heart and a discerning mind.

Readers love these books!

"*I can count on one hand* the amount of books I've read front to back in a day. These are so beautifully written, I can't wait for more to be released!"

~ Chantel Jameson-Farkas, Canada

"*Stunningly and beautifully written*, these are highly insightful books on the seven Chakras! I've heard the term Chakra before, but never connected it to the spine and its direct influence on one's body. I tried the breathing exercise and even began taking notes as I read through the books; there is so much useful information hidden in the stories!

On a personal level, the power of the chakras hit home as I began to make connections to my own life. The follow-up exercises made sense. From my personal experience in teaching children aged 9 to 11 years old, I believe that these books share very important life skills and should be included in school curriculums.

What you have created is very important, and frankly, for people of all ages. These books are fantastic, and I can see being a very important resource added to school libraries, both at the elementary and high school level."

~ Mark Desjardins, Canada

"*A beautiful, thoughtful, and magical journey* to exploring chakras. Embarking on a spiritual path feels inspiring, achievable, and understandable after reading these books. This is my type of education – fun and enriching to the soul! Truly a must-read for children, but arguably an essential read for all adults as well."

~ Poh, Canada

"*I am beyond amazed* at the talent and genuine beauty and creativity in these books! I learned so much about planting! I will be the first to order many books as this story will be legendary and already is in my world. Thank you and bless your heart for the information that you will pass on to kids and adults. May this help to impact the world in a beautiful way."

~ Mel Kiss, The Dominican Republic

A message from Yvette:

Thank you to all the healers, teachers, mentors, guides, family, and friends who have nourished my spirit and inspired growth. I have so much appreciation and love for you all!

Thank you to my nephews, Ethan and Lukas, who inspired this book series with their thoughtful questions during our many forays into the woods, countless hours in grandma's garden, the cabin, and bee yard, during our early mornings foraging for herbs, time spent lying in the thick, green moss watching the clouds float by and chatting, and of course, reading wonderful, uplifting stories each night after our meditations. It was great fun creating these stories based on many of our family adventures together, conversations, and heartfelt questions about some of life's mysteries.

My dear family, we have created and enjoyed many wonderful memories and moments together; my heart is filled with love, admiration, and gratitude for all we have shared. Thank you for supporting me in so many ways. I am very grateful to each and every one of you: Anyu, Apu, Otti, Attila, Katimama, Chantel, Nicole, Ethan, Lukas, Björn, Hudson, Bennett, Rollo, Gyuri, George, Ernestine, and our family dogs; Zserbo, Lui, Jake, and Moose.

Jutka, Misi, and Robi; I place you in the family category as that is what you are to me. Thank you for your neverending support and excitement about my various projects and adventures over the years. I feel blessed to have grown up with you in my life.

Carla Roter, I've had the pleasure and privilege of benefiting from your wisdom, love, support, and kindness for decades. Your unwavering belief in me and encouragement towards my dreams have meant the world. Through you, I've gained invaluable insights into compassion, witnessing firsthand how it can look when opening oneself to greater love and practicing non-judgment amidst life's challenges and triggers. Your constant support and presence have been a true blessing, profoundly impacting my life for the better. I've grown and learned immensely under your gentle guidance, through our honest conversations, and by observing your own graceful navigation through life's myriad "human moments." Thank you, dearest Kapha Mama.

Marcel; you bring so much joy, laughter, and inspiration to my life. You are one of those rare Souls who has the great capacity to hold a sacred space of incredible strength for me to relax into, supporting and empowering me to be my best and shine my light with the world from that space - a space of deep grounding, respect, care, appreciation, fun, and resilience. I love that you inspire me (and many others) with your own examples of growth and consistently strive for personal greatness. Thank you for being on this journey with me and for gently encouraging me to keep going and do what is important to my heart and Soul. I'm so glad you were "persistent." I feel blessed and excited to co-create this beautiful life with you.

Tom and Lilou, you have enriched my life with your shining Spirits, intelligence, humour, and sense of play. It excites me to see what your next amazing chapter of life will look like, and what beautiful gifts you will continue to bring to the world. Thank you for welcoming me into yours.

Deep appreciation and acknowledgement to all the guides who transmitted key information to be added to these books through dreams, visions, and synchronicities. The intent to have this uplift and empower its readers was obvious. This book series was a beautiful, collaborative co-creation between many that was joyful, easy, and flowed with love, wisdom, and clarity. I am honoured to have been a part of its transmission and excited to share it with humanity.

Jana, working with you in this creative playground has been an absolute pleasure. Your beautiful and clear energy, extensive professional experience, and incredible talent has elevated these books to new levels. What you have created is sheer magic and it excites me to know that many will have the benefit of enjoying your wonderful paintings and illustrations. You have brought many new ideas to the project and assisted in ensuring all the different pieces work synergistically well together. Deep gratitude to you for all that you are and all that you have brought and continue to share with the world. It has been an honour to take this path with you.

Thank you to my incredible writing partner, Wayne Bloemhof. You were the gift the Universe delivered when I made my request for assistance with this Soul project. Your ability to tune in to this vision, feel and deliver its essence, and work in harmony with me (and all our guides) was amazing. It was effortless and fun working with you. I am deeply grateful to you Wayne. You helped give these stories legs on which to stand. You truly are the "unofficial wordsmith for the River of Life," as you often say.

A big thank you to Juliana D'Costa who helped start the process of coming up with and creating the illustrations for these books. The countless hours spent laughing together, working in focused silence, and feeding off of each other's creative and "happy heart" energy was incredibly special. You provided so much positivity, clarity, and guidance that helped move this project forward. I love the frog illustrations - and all the others you did. You are incredibly talented my friend. All the good energy you have put into these books will be felt by its countless readers. What a special gift from you.

Thank you to my incredible user testing group. You read and re-read these books, providing valuable feedback, helping to ensure the information being shared made sense no matter the age or background knowledge of the reader. Your honesty and insight have made these books all the more easily received because you cared enough to dive deep into them, noticing loose ends that needed tying.

Sherri Mellamed		Juliana D'Costa
Poh Lin Cheng		Mark Desjardins
Shiren VanCooten		Maria Kiss
Nikolet Gárdián		Carla Roter
Éva Csuka		

Sincere gratitude to my outstanding editors; Poh Lin Cheng, Sherri Mellamed, and Bella Jasper. It was after your edits that I felt good about releasing this work to the world. The time you spent going through these books shows in the quality and final product. Thank you for helping to birth this inspired work with clarity and sincerity.

Hi everyone, I'm Ethan.

My aunt Yvette wrote some pretty awesome books about our family adventures. You'll like them.

My favourite book is the third one; in it, I am a bee who learns about "bee-things" and how to overcome self-doubt. That's something I've had to learn to do in real life too. I bet you can relate.

I'm the main character in these books, but you'll also get to meet my brothers, parents, and other family members. To help you remember who everyone is, I've drawn a picture for you. I like to keep things simple, so I made it a stick figure portrait.

I think kids and adults will all like these books. They feel good to read or have read to you, and you learn a lot of fascinating facts about things like using posture and breathing to help you feel more confident in life.

I hope you enjoy our family books!

Meet our *family!*

Aunt Yvette with Ethan, Lui (dog), Uncle Attila with baby Bennett,
Moose (dog), Aunt Nicole with baby Rollo and Björn, Ethan's Dad (Tom),
Ethan's Mom (Chantel) with Lukas, Grandma Suzan with Hudson,
Grandpa Otto, Jake (dog)

Welcome to Your Journey of Heart and Brain Harmony!

Dear friend, before we dive into the enchanting world of Ethan's story, let's embark on a special mission—one that involves the magic within you!

Take a Deep Breath

Close your eyes, take a big, deep breath in through your nose, feeling your chest expand like a balloon. Now, slowly exhale through your nose. Repeat this a couple of times, and notice how it makes you feel calm and centered.

Heartbeat Connection

Place your hand over your heart. Can you feel its gentle rhythm? As you slowly inhale and exhale, imagine sending love and kindness to your heart. Feel it glow with warmth.

Feel the Vibes

Smile as you imagine something or someone that helps you feel the warm hug of care, the loving touch of compassion, the upliftment of appreciation, and the cozy blanket of gratitude.

* **Care**
* **Compassion**
* **Appreciation**
* **Gratitude**

Let those feelings dance in your heart, creating a warmth that spreads throughout your body. Keep breathing slowly and deeply.

Empowerment Words

As you read this book, carry these potent words with you - "I am loved, I am appreciated, I am valued, I am cherished, I am smart, I am important, I am capable, I am confident, I am worthy, I am enough, and my heart holds incredible power." Whisper them when you need a boost of courage or a dose of self-compassion.

Smile and close your eyes again as you take another deep breath, feeling warm, loving energy permeate your body, soothing and relaxing you completely.

Wishing you an edifying journey filled with discovery and joy.

Crown Chakra
Third Eye Chakra
Throat Chakra
Heart Chakra
Solar Plexus Chakra
Sacral Chakra
Root Chakra

Note to parents and readers:

This is an introduction to the concept of chakras (pronounced "cha" as in "charge" and "kra."). It shows different ways of interpreting and approaching situations depending on what lens - or chakra - you are looking through. It contains many seeds of knowledge hidden "in plain sight" throughout the stories. When watered, these seeds will empower readers to intuitively guide themselves towards a deeper understanding and awakening of their own innate wisdom and potential.

The questions at the end of each section are designed to inspire meaningful conversation between you, dear readers and listeners. Use this opportunity to engage in thoughtful, heart-to-heart conversations, bringing you closer to one another as you make insightful connections.

Sacral Chakra

Creativity + Pleasure + Sense of Self

Enjoyment, expression, and how you relate to others and the world.

Sanskrit name: Svadhisthana meaning "The Place of the Self."

Location: Lower abdomen just above the pubic bone.

Colour: Orange

Element: Water

Focus: To feel

Sense: Taste

Bija mantra: VAM

A balanced sacral chakra:
- Easily relates to and connects with others.
- Enjoys taking pleasure in things such as eating, playing, and expressing yourself through the arts, sports or other creative ventures.
- You are flexible and easily flow with life, handling whatever comes your way.

Signs of imbalance:
- Anger, fear, fighting, guilt.
- Not comfortable opening up to people (doesn't make friends easily).
- Overly needy or dependent on people, routine, or things.
- Feeling numb with repressed emotions or hypersensitive and over-emotional.
- Feeling uninspired, bored, stuck, and uncreative.

Affirmations for the sacral chakra:
- I let myself have fun and be happy.
- I nourish my body with healthy food and clean water.
- I value, enjoy, and respect my body.
- I am bright and creative. I like making things.
- I enjoy connecting and sharing with others.
- I have great ideas and can create anything I set my mind to.

How to balance your sacral chakra:
- **Get creative!** Paint, draw, write a song, etc.

- **Have a heart-to-heart conversation** and hug someone you feel close with.

- **Breathe!** Get that energy flowing! Do the "ha breath" - inhale as much air as possible into your lungs while reaching high up towards the sky with both arms. Exhale powerfully sharply as you say the sound "HA!" and let your upper body fall down towards the ground hanging like a rag doll. Keep your legs straight and strong! Do this three times.

- **Move your body:** Play a sport, get on your bike, roll down a hill, get physically active to get your heart pumping and your energy flowing.

- **Get wet:** go swimming or take a hot/cold shower.

- **Wear orange** coloured clothes.

VAM

Finding Your Place on the Team:
Exploring the Sacral Chakra (Book 3)

Chapter 1:   What's it Like to Be a Bee...................................... 19

Chapter 2:   Stuck on the Bench.. 22

Chapter 3:   First, Bee Honest with Yourself............................25

Chapter 4:   Ethan's Gloomy Mood......................................29

Chapter 5:   When Feelings get in the way..............................32

Chapter 6:   Wumzie Magic Hands.......................................42

Chapter 7:   Aunt Yvetts's Roses.. 45

Chapter 8:   At the Threshold..50

Chapter 9:   A Shield of Golden Energy.................................. 58

Chapter 1: What's it Like to Be a Bee?

The first thing Ethan remembered about his dream was the loud buzzing. The droning noise filled his head and made him feel quite odd. His entire body reverberated with the sound. Everything he looked at seemed a lot bigger than it should have been. Floating in the air, all around Ethan, were hundreds of them.

So many bees! They were all buzzing around, going this way and that. Each bee was doing its own thing, and yet somehow, all of them knew exactly what to do and where to go. Not one bee bumped into another, even though they seemed to be flying in dozens of directions at once. It was quite dizzying to watch.

They had large dark eyes and hairy bodies with black and yellow stripes. It looked like they were wearing fuzzy flying pajamas covered in gold dust.

The strangest thing of all was that 10-year-old Ethan knew he was a bee too. Somehow, that made him very happy, and he smiled to himself.

"I must be dreaming," he thought, and then, just as he realized that it was a dream – lickety-split – he completely forgot again.

The bees were leaving the hive and heading towards a big open patch of sun nearby. Bee-Ethan sniffed the air.

There was an enchanting smell... sniff...sniff...

It was coming from where the warm, golden streaks of sunlight hit the patch of green just in front of a thick forest of trees. Everyone was heading that way. So, without even having to think about how or where to fly, Ethan flapped his bee wings like mad, and away he zoomed, following his nose, along with all the other bees, heading straight toward that delicious smell.

The trees looked enormous – like giant skyscrapers. They made his head spin when he looked up.

Far down below, a mile away, it seemed, there was a big, perfectly round, white and black object. It looked to be about the size of a big house. Ethan couldn't make out what it was, so he just followed the other bees. It was enormous fun, zigging and zagging all over the garden.

The flowers were as big as swimming pools. Something inside Bee-Ethan really wanted to go explore those flowers.

He saw a big, blue flower nearby. It had the most mesmerizing yellow spots on its petals. It looked like the other bees were having a party there. To his surprise, as soon as Bee-Ethan tried to join them, he found that he couldn't get there. He flapped and flapped – but it was no use. He was stuck. He just couldn't fly any closer.

Try as he might, he couldn't get to that tempting blue flower and the golden pollen party. The scene began to fade away. Something was calling to him. It sounded far away at first, then more insistent.

"Ethan!", came a loud call from downstairs, "you're going to be late for school. Get yourself down here!"

Ethan had overslept that morning.

He felt a little frustrated and disappointed when he woke up. He really wanted to join in the pollen party with the other bees.

Chapter 2: Stuck on the Bench

Ethan and his younger brother, Lukas, had soccer practice after school. Lukas, who played on the junior team, ran faster than others his age and loved showing off his skills with the ball. The coach selected him as the striker because nine times out of ten, Lukas could kick the ball straight into the back of the net.

The only thing the coach complained about was that Lukas didn't like to pass the ball to anyone else on the team. He was a soccer ball hog.

"You can't win the match on your own, Lukas," said the coach. "Soccer is a team sport. Pass the ball!"

Ethan, who was on the senior team, wasn't quite as sporty as his younger brother. He wasn't the fastest runner, and he had the habit of being too cautious. Ethan didn't like to take risks. He preferred reading books and drawing to playing sports. This year was the first time he had tried out for any kind of team, persuaded by his mom, who thought he should try something different and outside his comfort zone.

So far, things were not going his way. 'Different' was no fun.

There was a match coming up, and more than likely, Ethan would spend a lot of time on the bench again. The coach said he could try again in a couple of weeks and that he just needed more practice.

He tried very, very hard to fit in with the team. He always tried to be the kind of person he thought they would like, but still, he felt like an outsider. The other boys thought he was just weird, shy, and goofy. They actually believed that Ethan liked sitting on the bench. It was all a big joke to them.

Practice that afternoon was no different for poor Ethan. He was the last one over the finish line during the warm-up. He missed completely when it was his turn to kick a goal into the net. He couldn't stop the ball dead when someone passed to him, and it seemed like the coach was giving him a hard time.

The other boys on the team called him "Wumzie" (short for "Clumsy-Wumsy") because of the way he fumbled the soccer ball.

By the time the two boys got home, Ethan was in a foul mood.

Sacral Chakra Discussion Questions

1. What are some things you're really good at? Think about the things you enjoy doing and the ones you feel proud of. What skills or talents do you have?

2. What are some things you're still learning or working on? Are there areas where you feel like you could improve? What would you like to get better at?

3. How do you get along with other people? Do you find it easy to make friends and work with others? Are you part of any groups or teams?

4. Do you like being on a team? Why or why not? Think about how it feels to be part of a group. Do you enjoy working or playing with others, or do you prefer doing things on your own? Why?

5. Has anyone ever called you names? If so, how did it make you feel? What did you do about it?

6. Have you ever made fun of someone? If you have, why did you do it? How do you think it made the other person feel?

7. Have you ever encouraged someone who was feeling nervous or shy? Think about a time when you helped someone feel better about something they were worried about. How did that make them feel? How does it feel to help empower someone?

8. How do your parents and friends encourage you to do your best? What kind of support do you get from the people who care about you? How do they help you grow and improve?

9. How do you think other people see you? Do they think you're sporty, smart, creative, kind, or loud? After you answer, ask your parents and close friends to describe how they see you!

10. How do you see your parents? What kind of people are they? How would you describe your mom and dad to someone who doesn't know them?

11. Ask your parents these same questions.

Chapter 3: First, Bee Honest with Yourself

That night Ethan struggled to fall asleep. He ate far too many sweets after dinner. Usually, that was Lukas's thing. This time, however, it was Ethan. He was eating because he was feeling unhappy and useless. He indulged in a little too much honey. He had three big spoonfuls of the honey his Aunt Yvette harvested from their hives that summer.

When he finally did fall asleep, he dreamt that he was a bee again.

Maybe the bee dreams came to him because Aunt Yvette was a beekeeper, and he and his brother Lukas had spent the last two summers helping in the bee yard. They learned all about beehives and bee ways. They learned that bees make Royal jelly, honey, propolis, and beeswax. They saw how each hive had its own queen bee and how all the bees worked together as a team to create a happy, healthy, and harmonious family.

Whenever Ethan was in a bad mood, or if Lukas was angry, they weren't allowed into the bee yard.

The bees can sense your emotional energy. If you go near them when you are angry or upset, they react to that harsh, aggressive energy. It hurts them.

They know, and they protect their queen and the entire hive from disorienting, negative, disharmonious vibrations - including bad feelings.

Ethan knew that bad feelings also hurt people.

Aunt Yvette was in town that week to deliver honey and herbs from the farm. She was going to visit soon, and perhaps that's why Ethan was thinking about her.

Whatever the reason – this time, the bee dream was more of a nightmare. The other bees in his dream seemed cautious and suspicious of Bee-Ethan. Whenever he tried to fly towards one of them, they would disappear. When he tried to fly towards the beehive, he kept getting lost.

Finally, he just buzzed around a sad-looking flower that had lost most of its petals. He flumped down into the little bit of pollen still clinging there.

It was weird having six legs. Bee-Ethan tried wiggling them, one at a time.

"Weird," thought Bee-Ethan to himself, "I can feel the energy flowing in strange waves all around me and also inside my body. That must be my bee chi."

To his great surprise, the flower underneath his bee legs started to giggle.

"You're tickling me." It laughed. "Who are you anyway? Are you a real bee? How come you're not with the other bees?"

"They don't seem to like me," said Bee-Ethan sadly, and his sensitive feelers drooped down. "I don't know why."

"Maybe you're just imagining that they don't like you," replied the odd little flower with a big smile. It seemed way too cheerful. "And because you think that way," the flower said merrily, "you get tense, and your energy becomes all prickly."

"What does that even mean?" asked Bee-Ethan, huffing a big sigh. The flower was annoying him.

"Just Bee yourself!" laughed the flower – "But first, you have to be honest with yourself."

The cheerful flower began telling Ethan about the special relationship that bees and nature have.

"Look over there, past the big oak tree. There is a path with beautiful flowers along one side. Do you see it?" asked the flower. Bee-Ethan turned to look at the spot

"Yes, what about it?" wondered Bee-Ethan.

"Do you see how the flowers only grow on one side but not the other? None of the bees will cross the path to get pollen from those flowers either, even though they love those flowers. None of the animals will go there if they don't have to, and very little grows in that spot."

Suddenly, Bee-Ethan perked up with curiosity. His feelers straightened out as he stood up on one of the flower's petals, turning his bee body to look at the area the blue flower was talking about.

"Why don't the bees go there? It looks perfectly fine to me," wondered Bee-Ethan.

"There is a strong energy that flows there. It is very disharmonious and hurts all living things - even the humans who created it. They connect their electronics to this unnatural energy, but it hurts them and everything near it. That is why the bees and animals don't go there."

"If they get caught in that energy field, they can lose their sense of direction and can't find their way back home to their hive. Sometimes they even get sick. This unnatural energy disturbs the sensitive microbes, bacteria, and complex root systems underground that trees and other plants use to communicate with and support each other. Communication breaks down."

Bee-Ethan nodded slowly. He understood what the blue flower was telling him. He could see a large cell tower near the spot the flower pointed out. It produced something called disharmonious electric and magnetic fields (EMFs).

The next moment, Ethan was waking up. It was time to get ready for school again.

Chapter 4: Ethan's Gloomy Mood

"Lukas!" called his mom from the kitchen doorway, "Go and play somewhere else with that soccer ball! You're going to break the window."

Ethan's mom walked back across the hall and saw Ethan sitting by the table, drawing something.

"Your latest creation?" she asked – but Ethan just looked gloomy and didn't answer. The picture was of a bee – a scary-looking alien bee.

"It's from a dream I had," said Ethan, eventually. "But I can't remember all of it. There was this annoying, old flower. It kept bugging me."

"Really?" said mom, putting her arm around Ethan's shoulders. "I can't imagine a flower being annoying."

"Well, this one was!" said Ethan with a fuss and drew a big purple X over his drawing.

"Are you hungry?" asked his mom gently. "There are fresh blueberries from the farm, bread that your grandfather baked, and that jam you like so much."

Ethan wasn't interested.

"What's bothering you, kiddo?"

"Nothing," Ethan grunted angrily. "No one wants me to play with them! No one on the team wants to be my friend. I'm only good enough for the bench... sitting there all alone!" he stormed out of the room, covering his eyes with his arm to hide how upset he was.

Sacral Chakra Discussion Questions

1. Have you ever felt disappointed, sad, or that you weren't good enough?
   When this happens, how do you handle those feelings? What helps you feel better?

2. Do you think your parents or friends ever feel this way too? Ask them about
   times when they might have felt sad or discouraged. How did they cope with it?

3. Are you happy when you're by yourself? Do you enjoy spending time alone sometimes,
   or do you prefer being around others? Why do you think that is?

4. Have you ever felt like you didn't belong in a group or that you were an outsider? What
   did that feel like? Do you think other people feel that way too? Ask your friends if they've
   ever felt like they didn't fit in.

5. Have you ever tried to fit in somewhere new, such as a school or in a group?
   How did that feel? Was it easy or hard to make friends and feel comfortable?

6. What is it like to be new to a team or a class? Do you enjoy meeting new people, or does
   it take time for you to adjust? How can others help make someone new feel welcome?

7. Have you ever eaten so much that it made your stomach hurt? How did that feel? What
   do you think might happen if we eat too much, too quickly, or too late at night?

8. Have you ever eaten late at night and then had trouble sleeping because you were too
   full and your body was still busy digesting food? How does your body feel when you eat
   late? What do you think is a good time to stop eating before bed?

9. How much time do you usually leave between eating and going to sleep?
   Some people say we should stop eating at least four hours before going to bed. What
   do you think about that idea? Why is it important to give our bodies - including our
   digestive systems - time to rest?

10. Have you ever had trouble sleeping because your mind wouldn't stop thinking?
    Why do you think this happens? What can you do to calm your thoughts and relax
    before bed?

11. In what ways do you feel creative? Do you like to draw, sing, make things, or come up
    with new ideas? What creative activities make you feel happy?

12. In what ways are your parents creative? Ask them about their favorite hobbies or
    creative activities. If they could choose something fun and creative to do, what would
    it be?

13. Do you help out with chores at home? What do you think you could help your parents
    with? Is there anything you would like your parents to help you with?

14. Ask your parents these same questions.

Later that week, Aunt Yvette came to visit. She always brought fresh vegetables and fruit from the farm, and sometimes there was honey too.

If they were lucky, Grandma Susan would send honey cakes. Ethan's mom also baked many delicious pies, loaves of bread, and pastries. She was particularly famous for her butter tarts, and often made some when Aunt Yvette came to visit, since she knew how much she enjoyed them.

Aunt Yvette had to run some errands in town that morning and invited Ethan along, so they could talk. It took some convincing, but Ethan finally agreed. At least he would get out of the house for a while.

"Your mom and Lukas tell me you've been feeling down in the dumps," she began, but when Ethan didn't reply, she asked, "want to tell me about it?"

In a low voice, Ethan told Aunt Yvette about what was happening at soccer practice. "There's nothing I can do!" he complained. "What's wrong with me?"

Aunt Yvette thought about it for a moment and then replied carefully:

"There's nothing wrong with you, Ethan. Everyone is good at some things but not everything. That includes me, your coach, your parents, and every-one on your team. Many people are afraid to try things they don't think they are good at. Look at you, you told me you don't think you are very good at sports, yet you challenged yourself and tried out for the team. That was courageous of you."

"Maybe you need to look at things differently. Find new ways of learning the skills your coach is showing you. When I am learning something new and can't seem to get it, I try a different tactic, sometimes many new tactics. There's nothing wrong with that. Sometimes we learn by failing. That's ok too. Learning is different for everyone, and if you don't get something right away or it isn't something you are naturally good at, it doesn't mean you are useless. The trick is to find an approach that works for you, and that includes changing your mindset. If you believe you can, you can. If you believe you can't, well... you're right about that too."

"Do you even want to go to soccer anymore?" asked Aunt Yvette gently.

"Yes and no." Replied Ethan slowly as he mulled this over.

"I see how much fun the others are having as they play together, but they are all so much better than me, so I feel like an outsider, and that makes me feel sad and small inside. It feels like they don't want me either because I'm not as good as them." Explained Ethan quietly with his head down as a few tears slid out of his eyes.

"Instead of thinking that you have to do this, how about thinking that you get to do this, knowing that eventually, your skills will improve? Maybe you're harder on yourself than any of those other boys." Suggested Aunt Yvette.

"I don't think I'll ever be as good, no matter how much I try." Said Ethan sadly.

"Do you remember when my strawberry plants got sick? I talked to them all the time to encourage them and make them feel loved and appreciated. Of course, I also gave them more plant food and light. With the extra appreciation I gave them, they began to grow strong and healthy again. People are like that too. Sometimes we have to do that for ourselves. Keep encouraging yourself, Ethan, and go into the games expecting to have fun no matter how well you play. When someone radiates positive expectations, they attract a similar response from those around them. Just be yourself, little man, because you are awesome as you are. How about you focus on having fun instead?"

"You sound like that strange blue flower." Said Ethan as he stared out of he window.

Aunt Yvette wondered which flower Ethan was talking about but decided not to press the issue. Instead, she reminded him how bees react when you're angry and how they act when you are calm around them. She spoke to Ethan for a long time.

"Everything alive can feel the energy of everything around them. People are sensitive to thoughts and feelings too. If you feel bitter and angry, other people tend to avoid you – just like bees. If your bad feelings get in the way too much, you end up having arguments and making people around you unhappy."

"Do you remember what you learned about the chakras from Priya and her mom? That's the same energy I'm talking about. Your second chakra energy is all about how you connect to others and what kind of creative energy you bring to your own life. You feel it here in your belly."

"I can't help what kind of energy I have!" Ethan said defensively. "I can't help it! Everyone around me is being mean and making me feel bad."

"Actually, you can help it." Said Aunt Yvette gently.

"How you feel is not an accident. It's a choice. In life, there will always be things that don't go as you planned, and others may say or do hurtful things. We can't control that. What you can do is understand that it's not personal. You can also choose how to react. I'm not saying it's easy, but it really is that simple. Are you going to continue a spiral of negative feelings, or are you going to do something to change that energy?"

"I guess 'easy' and 'simple' are two very different things," said Ethan. "I know what you are saying, but it's really hard to do. I keep thinking about what happened over and over again, and it makes me feel so bad inside."

"You bring up a very good point, Ethan. Our thoughts are so powerful they can make us sad and even sick. Can you imagine that? Something that seems invisible, like our thoughts, have THAT much power. Tell me something, little man, who controls those thoughts?"

"Um... we do?" replied Ethan, half asking.

"That's right, and if the thoughts we choose to think can bring us down, they can also bring us up to feel joyful, content, or excited. You have the power to alter your inner world by the thoughts you think and the feelings you choose to focus on. You are in control. You make that decision."

"I guess I do tend to think a lot of unhappy thoughts." Admitted Ethan as he pondered their conversation. "It's a bad habit, I suppose."

"The good thing is that we can change our habits. A belief is a thought you keep thinking.[1] A habit is an action you keep doing. We can re-train ourselves and create new habits by changing our thoughts and behaviour. It takes practice, but you can do it. There is an exciting branch of science called epigenetics that explores this very concept. I'll tell you more about it another time."

Ethan, do you do yourself any favours when you keep on repeating the same unhappy conversations or scenes in your head for hours on end?"

"No, it doesn't feel good at all, but I don't know how to change my bad feelings when I get into a negative headspace." replied Ethan.

"Each one of us has to learn to redirect our emotional energies when necessary. When I feel upset, I do something to change the flow of that energy, so it

---

[1] Abraham Hicks (https://www.abraham-hicks.com/)

doesn't spiral down into a negative pit of anger or self-pity. I'll take a break and do something physical, like a speed walk outside in the forest, go for a swim or a long bike ride, put on music and dance my heart out, do breathing techniques, walk around and appreciate my garden, take an ice-cold shower, or exercise. There is nothing wrong with feeling down, as long as you don't let yourself get stuck in that feeling. Instead, make a decision to work it out and let it go."

"When you feel bad, don't bottle it up inside of you. That doesn't work, either. Allow yourself to feel your feelings fully, let them out, cry them out, hug them out, write them out, draw them out, or even scream them out if you are in an appropriate and safe space."

"The important thing is to acknowledge those feelings and let them flow through you. Don't pretend they aren't there or that you don't feel them. That doesn't help. You will feel lighter and better as you let out those heavy feelings. Choose new thoughts, tell yourself a new story about how the empowered, relaxed, and happy version of Ethan feels and acts in this situation, then redirect your focus and energy to THAT story."

Ethan wasn't convinced, but at least he was feeling a little better. Getting it out by talking through what was in his head, instead of keeping his emotions bottled up, shifted some of that stuck energy.

"Tell me more about your coach Ethan." Suggested Aunt Yvette.

"Well, as far as I know, he's been coaching for about ten years. He coaches several boys' teams and really likes what he does. He can be tough, though. I wish he would step in and tell the others not to be so mean sometimes."
"How are they mean?"

"They call me names because I can't play as well as them."

"Do they do this every practice?" Aunt Yvette asked Ethan.

"Well, no, not really, but even the odd time they do it, it makes me feel really bad. Actually, it's just one boy in particular, but the others laugh along with him. He is always on my case. Even in the changeroom he makes fun of me, getting the others to laugh. Whenever I miss a pass or goal, he says I am the worst player and that I'll never be good at soccer. I feel really bad, Aunt Yvette. It's hard for me to go back to soccer practice every week knowing that he is going to be there, waiting to pick on me."

Aunt Yvette and Ethan both sighed, then got quiet for a moment, each thinking their own thoughts.

"Ethan," Aunt Yvette began, "I understand how hurtful something like that can be. This is not your fault and it is not okay. Have you spoken with your parents and coach about this? What did they say?"

"No, but the coach must have noticed because he talked to me about it after our practice last week. He asked if I wanted him to talk with the boy's parents but I told him no. He walked straight over to the kid and gave him a lecture, telling him to quit it and improve his attitude, but privately, he still says mean things to me. I don't know why he picks on me, I've never done anything to him. The coach said if it doesn't improve, he will speak with the kid's parents. I told the coach to give me a few more weeks to figure it out on my own. I'm going to prove to them all that I am as good as any of them. I just need to practice more. Please don't say anything to anyone either!" Implored Ethan.

Aunt Yvette let out a long sigh. She now understood why Ethan was feeling so down lately. She also understood his need to handle things himself, however, she would still bring it up with his parents and see how they wanted to handle the situation.

"Ethan, you are amazing as you are and NEVER have to prove that to anyone. The only person you need to impress in life is yourself. That's it. Do your best in all that you do, but never confuse your self-worth with your ability to master a skill. Being good at something like sports or art is very different from being a good person, loving yourself, and feeling proud of the person you are."

Ethan was very quiet. Aunt Yvette could tell he was thinking about what she said, and needed time to digest the information and integrate it with his understanding of the world and his values.

In the meantime, she decided to brainstorm with Ethan further about his mindset.

"Ethan, is it also possible that you may be making this even more hurtful by thinking about it over and over again in your head?

Ethan went quiet for a moment. "I don't know, maybe… yeah, I guess I am making myself feel worse when I do that, aren't I?"

"You tell me, little man," smiled Aunt Yvette at Ethan gently.

Ethan sighed a long, ragged sigh and nodded a little as he admitted this was most likely true.

"Ethan, why don't you ask your coach to tell you about why and how he became a coach? Sometimes it helps to get to know another person more and understand them better. When you show genuine interest in people, they usually open up, often wanting to get to know more about you too. This may get the other boys interested in a new way of thinking, too."

They put their conversation on pause because Aunt Yvette had to finish delivering the herbs and fruit to the local market. She parked and got out, carrying several large, heavy boxes and a basket.

As she was climbing up a tall flight of stairs, some apples slipped out of the basket. Quick as a flash, Ethan caught two of them in his hands and stopped some of the others with his feet.

"Good catch!" laughed Aunt Yvette. "You should be the goalkeeper!"

"Hmmm, maybe I should be the goalkeeper. I am really good at catching things."

Ethan looked at the big, juicy, round apples in his hands…. and then he began to remember something from his dreams.

Sacral Chakra Discussion Questions

1. What does an emotion feel like? Can you describe some of the emotions you've experienced? For example, how does it feel to be happy, sad, excited, or nervous?

2. What kinds of thoughts do you have right before you feel really happy? What happens in your mind just before you feel excited or joyful? Can you think of a time when you were really happy?

3. What kinds of thoughts do you have right before you feel angry or scared? What thoughts or things happen to you when you're feeling angry or frightened? How do you usually respond?

4. Do you often think about the past or imagine what might happen in the future? Do you ever find yourself thinking about things that have already happened or worrying about things that might happen later?

5. What is the difference between self-confidence and self-esteem? Self-confidence is about believing you can do something well. Self-esteem is about how much you like or value yourself. How do you think these two ideas are different?

6. Have you ever felt bullied? If yes, when did it happen and how did it make you feel? How did you handle the situation?

7. Do you think it's possible to change the way we feel? Have you ever tried to change how you feel on purpose? For example, when you're scared or angry, have you ever done something to calm yourself down? What helped?

8. When you're feeling sad or lonely, what kinds of things make you feel better? Do you feel better after eating, exercising, getting some sleep, or doing something else? What kinds of things help you change your mood?

9. What coping strategies do you use to change how you feel? Ask your friends what they do to help change their mood when they're feeling down. Do you think those things work for them? Why or why not?

10. What's the difference between something being easy and something being simple? Can you think of something that is simple but not easy? Or something that is easy but not simple?

11. Ask your parents these same questions.

Dad was home.

He had been away in Newfoundland fixing an antique boat for a friend. He was an expert marine mechanic and had special requests far and wide. He didn't like to be away from his family, though, so he rarely took on projects far from home. The boys were happy to finally have him back and spend time with him.

"I know you've been doing a lot of fishing and gardening and frogging it up, but I think it's about time we got the soccer nets out," laughed dad. "How about we go and play a game or two while your mom and aunt are out?"

Soccer was a family tradition. Dad used to play for a team when he was younger and now enjoys getting together with other families on the weekend to kick the ball around. It certainly kept his fitness levels up!

"In Europe, they call soccer 'football'," dad said. "It can be confusing."

That morning the three of them went to the big park with a ball and spent the whole day having fun in the sun.

They set up a makeshift goal. Ethan wanted to practice his goalkeeping. He'd always been a player on the field trying to kick the ball into the net. This time he decided to put his quick reflexes to better use and try goalkeeping.

Lukas did his best to score as many goals as possible. He got about half the balls in the net, with Ethan managing to block the other half.

Then dad joined in and showed Ethan what to do.

"You're pretty tall with nice long limbs and quick hands," he said. "That's a good thing if you're a goalie. It suits your defensive nature. What do you say tomorrow we dig out my old goalie gloves?"

"The other boys call Ethan"Wumzie' at school," Lukas teased. "Clumsy Wumzie! It makes Ethan really mad."

"Well," laughed dad, as Ethan managed to catch the ball, "I think we will have to change that to 'Wumzie Magic Hands.' That's it, Ethan. Make sure you've got both hands on the ball. Keep practicing."

Later that night, dad brought out some vintage soccer videos with some of the best goalkeepers in the world. As they watched the game highlights, he showed Ethan some tricks and explained why the goalkeeper has to have a lot of courage.

"You're the final stop – nothing gets past you." He explained. "You have to imagine a brick wall in front of the goal and keep your eyes on the ball all the time!"

"What about imagining a golden wall of energy connected to my hands?" asked Ethan.

"That will help," agreed dad. "Why don't you try that next time? Look," dad said, pausing the video, "see how the goalie tells the defenders where to stand? See? He stands right by the goalpost when it's a corner kick."

Mom brought them some snacks and sat down between them. She was glad to see Ethan smiling again.

"How many new tricks has your dad taught you, Ethan?" she asked curiously.

Ethan thought for a moment, "six so far, mom."

"That's plenty. Master the basics and build your skills from there. I bet you will enjoy soccer practice a lot more next time." Ethan's mom smiled as she kissed him on the top of the head.

"So then," she added with a sly smile, "whose turn is it to wash the dishes?"

Chapter 7: Aunt Yvette's Roses

It was Ethan's turn to wash the dishes. "Mom," he complained, "we really need to buy a dishwasher."

"I have two already," replied Ethan's mom with a witty smile, "you and Lukas."

Aunt Yvette was sitting in the kitchen, telling them about her rose garden.

"Each year, when it's time to make rose jam and herbal remedies, I talk with the roses. I tell them my plans and invite the roses to work with me to help make medicines. I encourage them with my own energy and deep appreciation for the healing magic they bring to the world. It's a real team effort. We work together to co-create something wonderful."

"Do you think they listen to you?" asked Ethan's mom while reaching up for a jar of apricot jam on the top shelf.

"Of course, they do! In just a few days, they grow at least three times as many flowers, blooming and packed with healing rose essential oils and pollen."

"Isn't it just because of the fresh cow manure you mixed into their soil in the spring?" asked Ethan in a joking voice as he clinked the dishes.

Aunt Yvette laughed.

"Yes – you do have to feed them, that's true – but you know, when it's that time of year, nobody can believe how many flowers my rose bushes grow. There's more red than green on them. I love my roses!"

Ethan thought about that as he washed the dishes. After a while, he asked, "Do plants have chakras too?"

"That's a good question," said his mom while spreading a layer of apricot jam onto a slice of sweet bread. "What do you think, Yvette?"

"Well," she replied, "plants have a wide range of emotions, just like humans. Everything in this universe is a form of energy. Plants have a living pattern of energy, and they respond to whatever is around them. Animals too. Both plants and animals have feelings, though it may not be as obvious as with humans."

"So, do they have chakras or don't they?" Ethan asked again.

"I think they have their own distinct energy patterns. You can think of your chakras as train stations for energy trains. They are places in your body where lots of different tracks and trains of energy come together. There is energy everywhere and all through your body. At some places, the energy comes together, crisscrossing like all the different train tracks ending at the same station."

"Maybe plants have smaller energy train stations." Ethan's mom suggested as she began kneading dough for a big batch of ginger cookies.

"That's a good way of putting it, Chantel. I believe plants are a lot like us in some ways. They respond to appreciation and love as we do. They recoil and don't grow well when treated poorly or don't get enough sustenance. All of life is one big family of living energy. We are all connected in many different ways. Some are obvious, others less so, yet, we are all one in this vast web of life."

Ethan finished the dishes and turned to face his mom and aunt. "I had a dream that flowers and bees talk with one another. They know what each one is thinking at all times, even when far away from each other. They transmit frequencies. The flowers told me that when they sense bees about to start flying over to them, they produce more sugar and nectar, knowing that the bees will be there in a few minutes. Isn't that amazing?!"

"Yes, that is quite remarkable," replied his mom. "So flowers get sweeter the closer a bee flies to it?"[2]

"Exactly!" replied Ethan with a big smile. "I think that's awesome, mom! Talk about teamwork. Flowers give bees pollen and nectar, and bees help pollinate them. I mean… wow… just, wow."

"In my dream, I asked the flowers how they knew the bees were about to start flying over to them. They said they sense the vibrations and intentions of the bees. They don't even have to hear or see the bees. They simply know."

"To be honest, I feel a little like those flowers. I sometimes know things are going to happen before they happen. Does that ever happen to you, mom or Aunt Yvette?" asked Ethan quizzically.

His mom and aunt both nodded. "It happens to me all the time, Ethan," began his mom. "I always seem to know how you feel even before you get out of bed or get home from school. I usually have the phone in my hand, waiting for your call before it rings because I know you are thinking about calling me."

Everyone laughed at that because they knew it was true!

---

[2] Lilach Hadani from Tel Aviv University. (https://gardeninacity.com/2019/02/06/cant-you-hear-me-buzzing/) and David Sereda (https://www.davidsereda.co/innercircle)

Sacral Chakra Discussion Questions

1. Do you ever talk to trees or flowers? Do they talk to you?

2. Do you think plants and animals have feelings?

3. Do you have a pet? Can you tell how your pet feels? How so?

4. What do you think about energy? What is it? Where does energy come from?

5. Name the different types of energy you know about and give examples. (Some examples: Electromagnetic, electrical, chemical, thermal, mechanical, nuclear, sonic/sound, gravitational, biofuel, solar power, geothermal, wind energy, hydropower, piezoelectric, atomic, elastic, emotional energy, consciousness/thoughts/awareness).

6. What are some ways that we can use our energy? Think of your body, your feelings, and the thoughts in your head.

7. How is your body like an instrument? What parts translate the information and energy from your surroundings? How can you tune in to this information better?

8. How can you keep your body - your instrument - in tip top shape so it is in tune with nature?

9. How do you know if you are in tune with nature?

10. What may happen if you are out of tune with nature and her natural cycles?

11. Ask your parents these same questions.

Chapter 8: At the Threshold

That night in his dream, Bee-Ethan finally found his way back to the beehive.

He could hear loud buzzing coming from inside, and a round hole served as the door. In front of that door – wouldn't you know it – was a gatekeeper.

It was an enormous drone bee, and he was wearing what looked like goalie gloves on each of his six legs.

The drone looked a little like a police officer or a referee. It was some kind of keeper of the threshold.

Ethan wasn't sure what to make of it. He buzzed nearby, watching the comings and goings at the hive door. Whenever a bee would come to the opening, the drone would do an inspection first.

"I wonder if he will let me in?" Bee-Ethan thought. "I guess there's only one way to find out."

Carefully, Bee-Ethan approached. The drone held up two gloved bee legs.

"Halt! Who goes there?" asked the gatekeeper in a serious voice.

It was the strangest thing. Bee-Ethan couldn't exactly speak bee – but somehow, he felt like the drone could understand him, and he could understand the drone. The conversation – without using words – went something like this:

"Only those with official bee business and family members are allowed in! State the purpose of your visit!"

"Oh gosh, well, I'm not officially a bee – but I mean you no harm. I really love bees and honey – but don't worry, I won't take any of your honey."

"So... you're a tourist?"

"I guess…" Thought Bee-Ethan, using a shy sort of bee-body language.

The drone bee stepped up to him, sniffing Bee-Ethan, feeling his vibe, sniffing again, and then finally, he stepped back and nodded satisfactorily. "I don't smell danger, poison, sickness, or another queen bee on you. You have good vibrations - good feelings emanating from you, though you are a little on the shy side. Ok, you may enter." The gatekeeper's voice became more relaxed and inviting once he assessed Bee-Ethan to be of no danger to the hive.

"This way!" the drone said, using his feelers and his bug eyes to point the way into the hive.

And just like that – he was inside the hive.

"So it's true," Bee-Ethan thought to himself. "The right kind of energy really does open doors!"

The hive was an awe-inspiring place. Everywhere, for miles and miles it seemed, were trickles of sticky golden light and thousands upon thousands of six-sided hexagon openings called cells. It was bigger than a football stadium, or so it seemed to little Bee-Ethan.

There were drone bees and thousands of worker bees – and far up near the top, there was a most tantalizing light. The sound of buzzing was deafening, yet it felt so good to Bee-Ethan.

He flew up, up towards that honey-colored light, and there he saw the most radiant of all the bees – the queen bee herself.

"Wooooooow," sighed Bee-Ethan quietly in complete awe and enchantment.

"Welcome!" she seemed to be saying with her bee eyes. "Look at all my lovely children. Aren't they perfect and beautiful?"

"Yes," thought Bee-Ethan. "Each and everyone."

Bee-Ethan realized that what Aunt Yvette said about the hives being completely sterile, perfectly sealed with propolis, and constantly active - with each bee knowing exactly what to do - was right.

Fifty thousand bees worked in perfect unison - complete harmony - with each other. Thousands were flying around building hexagonal-shaped combs that would soon be filled with honey or a pip - a baby bee. Thousands more were flying in and out of the entrance to the hive, gathering pollen. A dedicated brood attended to the queen's every desire.

The queen was the hive's greatest treasure. The bees worked together as a team to protect, adore, and assist her. She gave them all life and created a radiant light, sound, and scent energy that connected every single bee in her family to each other. She maintained order in the hive through her complete harmony with the universe. When the queen was feeling good and in sync with nature's cycles, everything in her hive thrived.

"This is just like my human home," thought Ethan. "When my mom is feeling good, everyone feels good. When she is upset, we all feel on edge and out of balance."

Bee-Ethan was mesmerized by what he saw and felt from the queen bee and the hive. She emanated a sweet, enchanting scent that drew him to her. He instantly understood that everything she did was for the hive and the universe. Her life was one of service and joy. Her harmony with flowers, animals, plants, and all of nature was peaceful, deep, and profound. She could feel their unique vibrational signatures, identify every single blade of grass, navigate via the magnetic energy grid of planet Earth, know the cycles of the stars, the moons, and other planets far, far away, and live her life according to those cycles.

Bee-Ethan turned to one of the maiden bees near him and asked, "what language do you speak with each other? I hear lots of buzzing, and I seem to understand what you are all thinking, but how do you talk with one another?"

The maiden bee laughed with delight at the question. "Our language is made up of vibrations from light, scent, sound, geometric patterns, and feelings. Have you heard our bee songs?"

"Yes, you have many different songs, but I don't know what they mean," replied Bee-Ethan.

"Each song has a unique vibration that shares important information with other bees. Some songs tell the bees where to find flowers, others tell bees their hive is under attack, and some songs tell bees when someone is sick. There are also special songs that create harmony and healing in the hive." Replied the maiden bee while sealing a hexagonal cell with wax."

The maiden bee laughed in delight as she looked at Bee-Ethan, then began filling the next cell with honey.

"The most important song is the Song of Increase[3]. This song is sung when there is great health in the hive when the bees feel very strong, when there is plenty of food, and the bees are ready to multiply. It's a very special time,

[3] "Song Of Increase: Listening to the Wisdom of Honeybees for Kinder Beekeeping and a Better World" by Jacqueline Freeman.

and this is a very special song sung only when there is complete harmony within and without the hive."

"Bee-Ethan, do you smell the different types of aromas all around you? Do you feel the way light touches your bee body and how the tiny hairs on your body stand up like millions of little antennas when this happens?"

Bee-Ethan looked down at his bee body and saw many tiny hairs covering it. He nodded and said, "yes, I noticed these hairs would stand up straight sometimes or move in a specific direction, but I wasn't sure what it meant."

"Those little hairs are your antennae. They are a part of your sensory system. Your body can pick up lots of different types of vibrations - sound, light, scent, magnetic and electrical frequencies, and feeling vibrations - your body helps to translate them into meaningful information."

"Huh, you know what?" began Bee-Ethan, "my human body does the same thing. When we are scared or tense, the hairs on our arms and neck stand on end. Humans must have antennae on their bodies too."

"That's right," smiled the maiden bee as she flew over to the next hexagonal cell. "In fact, you have many more types of antennae than just your hair. It's also in the DNA of each cell of your body. They are coiled antennas that pick up, receive, and store all kinds of frequencies. The DNA receives, transmits, and stores information[4]. It also contains all the secrets of the universe - but few humans remember how to access that information. Most of your scientists call that "junk DNA" - but only because they don't yet understand how it works or how important it is. There is no such thing as "junk DNA." Every part of nature has an important role and is brilliantly designed by the Great Creator to work perfectly and in harmony with each other."

"We bees - and all of nature - understand what it means to be a creator in harmony with the universe. We remember one of the original creator languages made of light, sound frequencies, sacred geometry, and feelings such as love."

"We call that language Kelonta[5]. We use this language to create, connect, and bring life to everything around us. All bees can communicate in this ancient language, and all of nature understands it, too, because, at its core, it's all vibration frequency. Frequency is easy to decipher because your entire body was made to translate it."

Bee-Ethan realized the more time he spent with his new bee family, the more attuned he became to them and that he, too, began to understand this ancient language called Kelonta. He began to see the symbols of the sacred geometry all around him, feel the vibrations that the buzzing sounds the bee songs made as they bounced against and inside his bee body, and the information all the scents carried.

"So this is the original, primordial language of nature," thought Ethan to himself.

Bee-Ethan looked at the maiden bee excitedly! "I get it now! Everything is made up of frequencies, and our bodies and minds help translate those frequencies into information we understand!" That is the language! Vibrations are what make up the language!"

"That's right, Bee-Ethan," smiled the maiden bee. "Since everything has its own unique frequency, bees can smell, taste, and feel those frequencies. We can feel it if something is poisonous, sick, or has bad thoughts or feelings.

  [5] "Voyagers: The Sleeping Abductees" by Ashayana Deane

We can also feel love, health, safety, intent, and joy."

Bee-Ethan flapped his wings and did a happy bee dance. He was so thrilled with his newfound understanding. He realized humans also have this ability, but most have forgotten it. They tend to communicate by speaking instead of using their expanded senses, feelings, and awareness. They can feel and sense much more than what their five basic senses tell them. In fact, they can naturally sense more when they become very quiet and still inside of themselves and focus on their hearts.

"I knew there was more to my feelings and dreams." Thought Bee-Ethan to himself.

Chapter 9: A Shield of Golden Energy

The day that Ethan had been dreading – and at the same time, had been looking forward to – finally arrived.

It was soccer practice day.

Ethan saw his coach sitting by the front bleachers, adding air to the softer soccer balls with a pneumatic pump. He walked over to him and sat down. "Hi, Ethan; how's it going?" asked his coach as he glanced up from the air pump with a smile of acknowledgement.

"Pretty good," replied Ethan in a friendly tone.

"I was wondering, how'd you end up coaching soccer? Did you always want to do this?"

Ethan's coach smiled at the question, finished adding air to the last soccer ball, turned off the pneumatic pump, and faced Ethan.

"You know, you're the first person on this team to ask me that." Began the coach.

"Ask you what?" inquired one of the boys who happened to be running in their direction when he overheard part of the question.

"Ethan wanted to know how I became a coach."

"I want to hear this too," said another boy who was coming in from the changing room.

"Me too," said another as he ran over after seeing a couple of his teammates standing around the coach.

Pretty soon, the entire team gathered around Ethan and their coach.

"Well," laughed the coach, "I guess I'll tell you the whole story. It may not be what you expect, though."

"What do you mean?" asked the kid who usually called Ethan names during practice.

"I bet you were the all-star player, the one everyone wanted to be like, who scored most of the goals," continued the kid.

"Actually," replied the coach, "For the longest time, I was the worst player on the team."

"What?!" cried the boys in shock! "No way!"

They couldn't believe their coach had ever been a bad player. He was rated the number one coach in their district, there were waiting lists to get onto his teams, and he had played professionally at the college level before deciding to become a coach. He even worked as a volunteer during the off-season to run soccer clinics for those who couldn't afford regular soccer clubs.

"It's true," continued the coach. "For the longest time, I was the worst player on my team. I loved soccer; I just wasn't very good at it. My entire family played sports, so it was fun; however, I had no coordination or natural talent for the sport - for any sport, in fact. I was really clumsy."

The coach laughed, thinking back to his childhood days when he couldn't score a goal to save his life. "I remember feeling pretty badly about it at first, trying over and over again to catch balls passed to me, pass them back, get into the path of the ball, and the many drills I have you boys do - I was terrible at nearly all of them."

"I remember one particularly bad day where nothing seemed to go well, and the others had been making fun of me for it. We had a guest coach come out to watch us. He called me over to him and asked why I had signed up for the season. I told him that I really liked soccer even though I wasn't very good at it. He asked me what I liked about it. I told him that when I played with my family, it was awesome because we played together really well as a team, and it felt good to work cooperatively towards a single goal. When one person scored, we all felt great because we all won. It was a team effort. Yes, there was competition, but it was friendly."

"He then told me something that completely changed my attitude about playing with the others. Even though I didn't have natural talent, he said that it didn't matter because skills could be learned through diligent practice. What I did have, however, was a good head for strategy. He saw that when I played, I would figure out the best positions from which to pass or line up a shot and went for it. It was like I had a game plan in my head about the many different possible ways to win."

"He told me while everyone thinks about how best to score a goal, not everyone could think out multiple strategies on the spot the way I did. You know what? He was right. I was always thinking about who would be best where and when based on their skills and temperament. I was already thinking like a coach even though I didn't know it at the time."

"He then gave the entire team some pointers for building their skills. He broke it down using a different teaching method. It was a method that worked for me. Right then and there, I decided to keep going to soccer practice and think about it as a fun exercise - like when I played with my family."

"I knew that eventually I would get better and focus on that end goal to keep a good attitude during the days when things didn't go well. Sure, there were days when I felt frustrated and had to go for a hard bike ride or swim after practice to calm down, but I kept practicing, and eventually, my skills did improve."

"I also took notes on top game strategies by watching world competitions and reading the best books on the subject. My sister was a champion chess player, and she did the same thing - she studied the winning strategies of the top chess players in the world. She and I both studied a lot - her with chess and me with soccer. As my confidence grew, so did my own suggestions for strategy, which I began to write down in a blue notebook, complete with full game plans, diagrams, and even the names of my teammates with their top skills and suggestions for improvement."

"One day, towards the end of the year, my coach at the time happened to catch me writing in my blue notebook as I was watching one of my team-mates practicing a particular drill. He came over to see what I was doing. I showed him my book, which was packed full of game plans, pointers, and even new ideas on how to teach various drills to help different types of learners. He was impressed and suggested that next year I enroll in their special coaching program that the club was going to start up."

"That, boys, is where things took off. I found my stride as a player by changing my attitude and finding different ways to learn while I kept practicing. Some of the other boys on my team even began asking me for tips when they saw me trying out new drills I had invented because they saw how much I had improved. Do you have any idea how good that felt? To be asked for advice from the same kids who made fun of me a year earlier? In the end, we became good friends. Who would have thought?" He smiled, thinking of his friends and the tight bond they had forged over the years, despite the bumpy start.

"The next year in the special coaching program, I discovered how truly passionate I felt about teaching. It brought me tremendous satisfaction helping others improve, gain confidence, learn new skills, and become better human beings in a positive environment doing something fun. I like empowering people and seeing them improve. It feels good."

"It's not always easy, especially if you aren't naturally gifted, but don't ever let that stop you from following your passion."

"I would never have guessed you weren't a great player, coach." Said one of the boys as they all pondered what their coach had revealed to them.

Ethan was deep in thought. He had made a decision before showing up to practice that day. He would take a different approach based on his skills, temperament, and learning style. He took out the goalie gloves his dad had given him and quietly put them on.

"Hey, Wumzie, why are you wearing those gloves?" asked the biggest, meanest boy on the team. "Are your hands cold? Need a blanket?

Everyone laughed. "Wumzie, the weirdo!

Ethan felt the same old bad feelings starting to come back. Why were they so mean to him? Was it always going to be like this?

Then he remembered the lessons he had learned about the second chakra. He thought about what his dad had said – how a goalie needs courage. He also thought about what his coach had just told them.

Taking a deep breath, he decided not to get upset again. It wasn't easy, but he gave it his best shot.

"I want to try out for goalie," he said and looked the mean boy straight in the eyes.

The other boy looked surprised. Never before had Ethan stood up to him.

"Take it easy, boys!" warned the coach. "Tell you what – why don't we do some penalty shot practice? Ethan, you're in the goals. The rest of you line up behind the penalty spot."

Ethan took his place on the goal line, and he gathered up every bit of courage he could muster. Remembering his lessons, he imagined a brick wall made out of golden energy all the way across the goalmouth.

The first boy stepped up to the ball and took a shot – but the ball went wide and missed.

"So far, so good," thought Ethan as he concentrated on keeping his knees
from knocking together; he felt so nervous.

One after the other, the boys on the team took shots at the goal. One after
the other, Ethan caught the ball or pushed it over the top of the crossbar. Out
of eleven boys, only two managed to score a goal.

The final one to take a shot was the big, mean boy who had teased Ethan
the most.

He sneered. "Get ready, Clumsy Wumzie!
Prepare to meet your doom!"

The shot came in high and fast – like a whizzing black and white bullet.
The ball headed right for the top corner of the net, but Ethan was watching
it like a hawk.

At the last moment, he jumped with all his might and managed to get his
fingertips onto the edge of the ball. It was enough to push it out of the way.
The ball pinged off the crossbar and up into the air - missing the net!

Saved!

All the boys cheered!

Several even patted him on the back, saying things like "good job Ethan" and "great save!" The boy who had been the meanest slowly walked over to him with a strange look on his face. He stopped walking when he was standing directly in front of Ethan and simply stared at him for a moment.

Suddenly, he smiled as he brought his hand up to "high five" Ethan and congratulated him on the save!

Ethan felt elated, and just like that, he finally felt he had clicked with the rest of the team.

Ethan had proven himself and earned his spot as a goalie on the team. Most important of all, Ethan had proved himself to himself. The hardest parts were to keep showing up, make a decision about the position he most wanted to play, have the courage to go for it despite pushback, and stand up to the bully.

He also began to understand how learning to maneuver his thoughts and emotions better was similar to learning how to maneuver the ball and the dynamics of a team.

Ethan felt a huge weight drop from his shoulders. He completely relaxed, smiled for the first time since the first soccer practice weeks ago feeling great about himself, then jogged back to the penalty spot with the ball.

"Boys," said the coach. "It looks like we have a new goalie. You'll have to give him a new nickname. What do you say?"

"Nah," replied Ethan with a grin, "I kind of like the name 'Wumzie!' I think I'll keep it."

"Wumzie!"
"Wumzie!"
"Wumzie!"

Yelled the boys in unison to cheer him on, only this time, instead of it stinging, Ethan felt a newfound sense of belonging with his team that made his heart sing with pride and joy.

The End

What Do You Think About The Third Book?

Friends, we have come to the end of book 3.
How did you like it? What did you most enjoy about the story?

I'd love to hear about your favourite parts and welcome you to
share them with me via email at: feedback@singingsoulbooks.com

As a gift to you, dear reader, here is a sneak peak of the first two chapters
of book 4. Enjoy!

Loving appreciation to all that you are and bring to the world.
Keep shining your light!

Warmly,

Yvette

Book Four:
Finding Your Own True Path
Exploring the Solar Plexus Chakra

Chapter One: An Adventure in the Rockies

"Gasán uu dáng gíidang? Bonjour and hello, how are you?" asked a friendly-looking woman wearing colourful clothes standing by the forest path. She was going to be their guide. She smiled warmly and invited everyone to come closer.

"Welcome! My name is Ts'áak," she said, "which, in the Haida language, means Eagle."

She shook everyone's hands and looked each one in the eye as she greeted them. "Are you folks ready to go? Come on, let's walk – we have a long way to go this morning. Don't forget your drums if you have them!"

The group set off into the woods.

"This is one of my favourite places in the entire world," Ts'áak explained as they all headed down the path. "To my heart and my eyes, it is the most beautiful place in the world. I'm happy to show it to you."

Ethan looked around. It really was breathtaking.

The snow-capped Rocky Mountains towered up into the clear sky and far down below were crystal clear lakes. They were blue, like husky eyes, and so peaceful. Tall trees and green ferns covered the slopes, and the crisp mountain air carried the scent of fresh pine needles.

They were up in the mountains of Western Canada by the Pacific Ocean. Ethan, Hudson, and Lukas were with their dad, Tom, as well as cousin Björn and his dad, Attila. There were also a few other people that they didn't know. A couple of them had brought hand-made drums of their own.

The boys had been looking forward to this hiking trip all year – it was going to be an adventure to remember.

It was still very early in the morning. They were all going to hike up to the sacred caves that overlooked the valley. There, they would participate in a drumming circle and a traditional cleansing ceremony. Lukas had been practicing his drumming for weeks now – and, of course, that had annoyed Ethan and Hudson to no end.

Secretly, Ethan was a bit afraid of making a fool of himself while playing the drum. He felt ashamed because he believed that he had no rhythm and thought he would never learn since he kept messing up.

Soon enough, though, he forgot all about that as they walked high up into the hills. All around them, only the pure sounds of nature could be heard. Everyone felt immense energy and awesome power all around them. It was truly a special and sacred place.

Chapter Two: The Spirits of Nature

All morning they hiked up into those magnificent mountains. They came to a rickety hanging bridge that spanned a deep gorge. It was a very long way down, which frightened Hudson. Björn didn't want to go across either, but Lukas, as usual, was feeling brave and wanted to show off.

"You're such a scaredy-cat, Björn," he teased with a sneer, "I'll go first!" and without even checking that it was safe, he rushed onto the bridge. But as soon as he stepped on, it began to sway under his feet. Lukas cried out and grabbed hold of the ropes.

Ts'áak, the guide, was instantly there to help him, "take it easy, my brave young wolf cub! Don't be reckless. Rushing into a place you do not know can be dangerous."

"Sorry," murmured Lukas, looking both dejected but relieved that he was safe as he hurried back to his dad.

Tom carried Hudson across. Björn and his dad, Attila, went next, "Don't worry, son," said Ethan's uncle Attila. "Take my hand – I've got you. We'll go across together." Björn looked terribly unhappy. His feelings were hurt because of what his cousin had said, but Lukas didn't even seem to notice.

When it was Ethan's turn to go across, he felt very unsure of himself too, but he didn't want his father to hold his hand or the others to make fun of him, especially since he was the oldest of his siblings and cousins.

So, gripping the ropes tightly with both hands, he took a few careful steps. Halfway across, he looked down, and he felt butterflies in his stomach. He closed his eyes and held on tight. It took all his courage just to open his eyes again, but when he finally did, he saw something amazing.

"Look!" he yelled, "down there!"

Far below them, they saw a great big black bear catching fish in the stream. "You have good eyes," said Ts'áak. "Well done, Ethan!"

Ethan felt a little better about himself, but now the shoe was on the other foot, as they say, and Lukas started feeling jealous of his big brother. As they continued on the path, everyone could see that Lukas was angry. He had been walking right behind Ts'áak with everyone else behind them all along, but now he walked at the back with a look of annoyance on his face.

Later they saw otters, elk, caribou, and moose, and Ts'áak found what looked like the tracks of snowshoe hares and even a lynx. As they walked, she told them all kinds of things about the animals they saw, pointing out their tracks, the various mushrooms and berries along the way, and telling them the names of the birds as they heard different chirps and whistles. She was a wealth of information, with knowledge pouring out of her! Ts'áak seemed to know what every single plant and animal in the area was called and also what was special about each one.

"My people believe that nature is alive and aware of us, constantly watched over by the ancient spirits, and that is why we must live in the right way. The stories of our tribe teach us how to be humble, wise, and respectful with each other, ourselves, and the world. This "right attitude" helps us to find the path of the heart and live in harmony within ourselves and each other."

Björn was very interested, and he asked all kinds of questions. Ts'áak smiled and patiently answered all of them. She said: "We humans are meant to be the protectors and keepers of nature, of our world. The animal guides can help show us the way. They each have their own lessons about how to do this. Each animal has its own unique gifts that it brings to the world. The may choose to share these with us humans if we prove ourselves worthy of that knowledge. But first, we must be clear and humble enough and have an open heart before we are ready to hear their message. Tonight, in our drumming circle, you may get to meet your own spirit animal if your heart and intent are pure enough."

An excited murmur swept through the group, as many considered this to be one of the highlights of the trip. It was a very special and sacred connection and one that many were eager to know more about.

Björn replied that he already had an animal guide – the grey owl.

Ethan became very thoughtful as he walked.

To be continued...

Sacral Chakra Song for Children

Sacral Chakra, I create,
Joy and laughter, oh, so great.
Orange like the sunset sky,
With my feelings, I can fly.

In my belly, bright and warm,
A lovely light, it keeps me calm.
Sacral chakra, orange and bright,
Creative power, pure delight.

Dancing rivers, flowing free,
My sacral chakra, joy for me.
I sing "VAM," and feel the cheer,
With my heart, I have no fear.

Svadhisthana, I'm alive,
In my flow, I strive and thrive.
With my feelings, I express,
In this space, I feel my best.

VAM, I chant, it makes me shine,
Creative energy, so divine.
I am joyful, I am free,
With my sacral, I can be me.

Sacral Chakra, I create,
Joy and laughter, oh, so great.
Orange like the sunset sky,
With my feelings, I can fly.

Yvette Farkas

Yvette is the creator of Singing Soul Books and a magical story enchantress. She can often be found wandering the deepest sanctuaries of forests and mountains and enjoying the "thundering loud" quiet of sacred spaces both outside and within.

She enjoys sharing her love of the unusual and mystical such as bullwhip cracking, foraging for herbs while the dew is still fresh, harnessing the power of natural energies, telling captivating stories in her yurt, and sharing wisdom gleaned from 30+ years of training in the martial and healing arts.

Yvette is an explorer of consciousness, a writer, gardener, photographer, traveller, and a budding beekeeper. She is a child of the Universe, leaving seeds of joy and the sweet aroma of empowered belief in the people she meets while learning and growing.

Yvette is also a health-based, heart-centered coach and mentor, and a practitioner of ancient healing practices taking people back to their health and their hearts. She uses the power of stories to share love and wisdom and reveal the inherent interconnectedness of all things, inspiring and empowering others toward their highest potential. Her work is meant to shed light on that which people rarely see, to uplift their Spirits, forge deep heartfelt connections, and inspire their hearts.

You can reach Yvette here:

www.singingsoulbooks.com, www.yvettefarkas.com and www.bioresonancescans.com
LinkedIn: https://www.linkedin.com/in/yvettefarkas

Jana Rothwell

Jana is the illustrator of Singing Soul Books. She finds passion in using her endless imagination to teach and create art that captivates people of all ages. She strives to empower others to grow, to learn to love themselves unconditionally, to speak their truth and to follow their dreams. She enjoys exploring the beauty in nature and feels most at home near and in the water. Jana encompasses all the characteristics of a typical Pisces: she is creative, gentle, sensitive, kind, compassionate, intuitive, and wise. Infinite amounts of light and love radiate from her. She connects deeply with children and animals because of their innocence and pure hearts.

She has the unique ability of seeing the best and the potential in everyone she meets. As a strong believer in the vastness and power of the Universe, Jana embraces the idea that we are all connected. She is a free spirit, continually learning and growing, always ready to share her creative ideas and stories, and never afraid to laugh at her own silliness.

You can reach Jana here:

janarothwelldesigns.com
Email: info@janarothwell.com
Instagram: @janalee_111 and @marigold_artstudio

Wayne Bloemhof

Wayne is a piece of the infinite creative wonder that just is. He claims nothing special as his own, always amazed at the words that come out of his fingertips as he types. Where do they come from? We can only speculate.

He lives in a place called Knysna, which is a little piece of heaven. He feeds the Turacos and white-eyes, sharing his apples, oranges and bananas with the forest creatures.

He often just walks down to the river, for no reason in particular, and leads a quiet life of wonder. He writes, ghostwrites and creates to help people put words to the stories in their hearts.

You can reach Wayne here:

www.waynebloemhof.wordpress.com
Email: waynebloemhof@gmail.com

Resources

Glossary.. 79

Palachinta Recipe 82

The Mystic's Library of Excellence 84

    Mind and Practical Metaphysics.......................... 84

    Consciousness, Quantum Physics, and Epigenetics.................... 87

    ESP, Remote Viewing, Quantum Physics, and Consciousness Expansion.................... 89

    Soul Matters, Past Lives, Dreams, Reincarnation, and Near Death Experiences.................... 91

    Parthenogenesis and the Divine Feminine.................... 92

    The Alpha Male and Divine Masculine.................... 94

    Communication Styles of Men and Women.................... 95

    Taoism and Inner Alchemy.................... 96

    Martial Arts Philosophy.................... 98

    Shamanism and Psychedelic Plants.................... 100

    Health (Wholeness) and Healing.................... 101

    Yoga Philosophy 107

    Ayurveda (The Science of Life).................... 109

    Sacred Geometry and Physics.................... 110

    Finances and Wealth.................... 111

    Behaviour and Body Language.................... 113

    Transmitted and Channelled Information.................... 113

    Conscious Leadership, Mentorship, and Coaching 115

    Other.................... 116

    Devices for Health and Healing 118

Glossary for the third book:

Spiritual, metaphysical, and unusual terms and their meanings from the third book in the "Ethan and the Seven Chakras" book series.

1. **Bee Chi:** A playful term referring to the energy flow within a bee, emphasizing the interconnectedness of living beings and their energies.

2. **Beekeeper:** A person who keeps and tends to bees, often collecting honey and other bee products, emphasizing Aunt Yvette's role in the story.

3. **Bench:** In sports, the substitute players' seating area; also used metaphorically to represent being on the sidelines or excluded from active participation.

4. **Bottle up:** Suppress or restrain one's emotions, often not expressing true feelings outwardly.

5. **Chi:** In traditional Chinese culture, the vital life force that flows through all living things, often associated with energy and balance in the body.

6. **Clumsy-Wumsy:** A nickname given to Ethan by his teammates, highlighting his perceived clumsiness on the soccer field.

7. **Colloquial:** Informal language or expressions used in everyday conversation, specific to a particular region or group of people.

8. **Comfort Zone:** A situation or environment where someone feels safe and at ease, often used in the context of trying new experiences or activities outside this familiar zone.

9. **Co-create:** To create or produce something collaboratively with others, emphasizing joint effort and shared creativity.

10. **Consciousness:** The state of being aware of and able to think and perceive one's surroundings, often associated with self-awareness and thoughts.

11. **Droning:** A continuous low humming sound, in this context, referring to the sound created by the bees.

12. **Disharmonious:** Lacking harmony or agreement, indicating the disruptive and negative nature of certain energies on living beings and ecosystems.

13. **Drooped:** Hung down or bent downward, indicating the sad posture of Bee-Ethan's sensitive feelers when he felt rejected by the other bees.

14. **Dumps:** A colloquial term for feeling sad or depressed, often used to describe a low emotional state.

15. **Drone Bee:** Male honeybee whose primary function is to mate with a fertile queen bee.

16. **EMFs (Electric and Magnetic Fields):** Electromagnetic fields produced by nature such as the sun and stars, and disharmonious ones created by electronic devices and cell towers.

17. **Enchanting:** Delightfully charming or captivating, describing the smell that attracted the bees and, metaphorically, representing its alluring nature.

18. **Epigenetics:** The study of changes in organisms caused by modification of gene expression rather than alteration of the genetic code itself, highlighting the impact of environment and experiences on genetic traits.

19. **Foul Mood:** An irritable or bad-tempered state of mind, indicating Ethan's negative emotions after the soccer practice.

20. **Indulged:** Allowed oneself to enjoy the pleasure of, often in excess, describing Ethan's action of eating too much honey due to his emotional state.

21. **Kelonta:** An ancient language made up of light, sound frequencies, sacred geometry, and feelings, according to Ashayana Deane. It represents the original language of creation according to the narrative.

22. **Make-shift:** Acting as a temporary and usually less satisfactory substitute; improvised.

23. **Marine Mechanic:** A skilled technician specializing in repairing and maintaining marine vehicles, especially boats and ships.

24. **Mesmerizing:** Captivating or fascinating, describing the effect of the yellow spots on the blue flower.

25. **Microbes:** Microscopic living organisms, such as bacteria and fungi, often essential for the balance and health of ecosystems.

26. **Metaphorical:** Symbolic or representative, used to describe language or expressions not meant to be taken literally but to convey a deeper meaning.

27. **Mulled:** Thought about deeply and at length, often used to describe a person pondering or reflecting on a situation.

28. **Outsider:** A person who does not belong to a particular group or community, often feeling alienated or isolated from others.

29. **Piezoelectric:** A type of energy conversion in which mechanical stress is transformed into electric energy, or vice versa, in certain crystals or ceramics.

30. **Primordial:** Existing at or from the beginning of time; ancient or prehistoric.

31. **Propolis:** A resinous substance collected by bees from tree buds and used to seal cracks and gaps in the hive. It has antimicrobial properties and helps maintain hive hygiene.

32. **Prickly:** Feeling uncomfortable or irritated, often used metaphorically to describe a person's energy or demeanor.

33. **Quizzically:** In a questioning or puzzled manner, often used to describe a facial expression indicating confusion or curiosity.

34. **Radiates:** Emits or gives off, often used metaphorically to describe a person's energy or aura.

35. **Reflexes:** Automatic and often rapid responses of the body to particular stimuli, often used to avoid danger or respond to sudden situations.

36. **Recoil:** To draw back or shrink in fear, disgust, or alarm; to react negatively to a situation or stimulus.

37. **Reverberated:** Echoed or resounded, indicating the vibrating sensation felt throughout Ethan's body due to the buzzing noise.

38. **Sacred Geometry:** The belief that geometric shapes, ratios, and patterns have symbolic meanings and are inherent in the natural world. It often involves the study and use of specific geometric shapes in religious or spiritual contexts.

39. **Vibrational Signatures:** Distinctive patterns of vibrations that are unique to each living being, object, or element in nature.

40. **Zigging and Zagging:** Moving quickly in a series of sharp turns or changes in direction.

Palachinta Recipe (spelled "palacsinta" in Hungarian)

Curious to taste the delicious dessert that Grandma Suzan made Ethan and the kids in the story? Here it is! Make these special Hungarian crepes yourself and share them with your loved ones.

These pancakes are large in diameter and very thin, unlike their North American cousins which are smaller in diameter yet thick.

The thin size of Hungarian crepes enables you to spread jam, cottage cheese, chocolate, nuts, or other foods on the crepe, and then roll it up for eating. You can also pour maple syrup, freshly made chocolate sauce, or other treats onto the rolled-up crepes.

Equipment:

- Mixing bowls
- Measuring cups
- Whisk
- Non-stick frying pan
- Spatula
- Fork
- Ladle
- Plates

Ingredients:

Batter
- 2 whole eggs
- 1 1/4 cups all-purpose flour
- 1 1/4 cups almond, oat, or other milk
- 2/3 cup sparkling water
- 1 pinch salt
- 1 teaspoon sugar
- Oil/fat for frying

Cottage cheese filling:
- 1 egg yolk
- 2/3 cup dry cottage cheese or ricotta
- 1/2 lemon zest
- 1 teaspoon vanilla extract
- 1 tablespoon sugar
- Mix, spread on crepe, roll up, and eat.

Walnut filling:
- Ground walnuts
- Sugar
- 2:1 ratio of walnuts to sugar (some people prefer a 1:1 ratio, adjust to your preference)

Instructions:

• Mix all ingredients except the
  sparkling water. Ensure there
  are no lumps in the batter.

• When smooth, add the
  sparkling water and mix.

• The consistency should be
  similar to that of a yogurt drink.
  Not too runny yet not thick.

• Set a frying pan over medium heat.
  Add a few drops of oil. Once hot, fill the
  ladle with batter and pour it evenly onto the
  frying pan.

• Tilt the pan in all directions so the batter coats the surface of the pan
  completely. If you have holes in the palachinta, fill them with a little batter.

• Fry the underside of the palachinta until it is a light golden brown colour.
  Use a spatula to loosen it from the frying pan and check the underside to
  be sure it is a golden colour.

• Flip the pancake and fry the other side as well. When done, slide the crepe
  onto a plate and prepare the pan for the next ladle of batter.

• Stir the mixture each time before pouring it into the pan.

• Repeat until you have used up all the batter.

• Spread each pancake with jam, walnut filling, or cottage cheese filling.
  Roll up and enjoy eating with friends and family.

The Mystic's Library of Excellence

The Mystic's Library of Excellence is a treasure trove (organized topic-wise) for those seeking to dive deeper into the ideas explored in the "Ethan and the Seven Chakras" books.

Topics include sacred geometry, remote viewing, near-death experiences, longevity practices, divine feminine and divine masculine concepts, championship mindsets, epigenetics, practical metaphysics, natural health practices, parthenogenesis, quantum physics, shamanism, energy medicine, ESP, and finance smarts.

For a detailed list with links, visit: www.singingsoulbooks.com

Each topic is a gateway to understanding the profound and the extraordinary. May your exploration be edifying and enriching.

Mind and Practical Metaphysics:

1. **Dr. Joe Dispenza**

    • **Books:** *Breaking the Habit of Being Yourself, Becoming Supernatural* (and other books)

    • Dispenza's work focuses on neuroscience, epigenetics, and quantum physics. His programs, books, and retreats guide people to elevate beyond their old patterns and create new ones toward a healthy, happy life.

2. **José Silva**

    • **Book:** *The Silva Method*

    • Silva's landmark work uses hypnosis and mental training to awaken the human mind's hidden potential beyond the traditional five senses.

3. **Florence Scovel Shinn**

    • **Books:** *The Game of Life and How to Play It, Your Word is Your Wand, The Secret Door to Success, The Power of the Spoken Word*

    • Emphasises the power of positive thought, affirmations, and spiritual principles for success and fulfilment.

4. **Esther and Jerry Hicks**

   • **Books:** *Ask and It Is Given: Learning to Manifest Your Desires, The Astonishing Power of Emotions: Let Your Feelings Be Your Guide* (and other books)

   • Explores the law of attraction and provides practical guidance on manifesting desires.

5. **Zinovia Dushkova**

   • **Book:** *The Secret Book of Dzyan: Unveiling the Truth About the Oldest Manuscript in the World, Revelations of the Sun, The Teachings of the Heart* (and other books)

   • Renowned author and philosopher, Zinovia Dushkova, Ph.D., was named one of the "100 Most Spiritually Influential Living People in 2020" by Watkins Mind Body Spirit magazine. She has written over 60 books, inspiring readers with her profound insights into love, compassion, and spiritual transformation.

6. **Neville Goddard**

   • **Books:** *The Power of Imagination*

   • Goddard's work delves into the transformative power of imagination and how it shapes our reality.

7. **Joseph Murphy**

   • **Books:** *The Power of Your Subconscious Mind*

   • Murphy explores how the subconscious mind influences behaviour and offers techniques to harness its power for personal success.

8. **Napoleon Hill**

   • **Books:** *The Law of Success in Sixteen Lessons, Think and Grow Rich* (and other books)

   • A classic in personal development, Hill's book outlines principles for achieving success and wealth through positive thinking and goal-setting.

9. **Dale Carnegie**

   • **Books:** *How to Win Friends and Influence People*

   • Carnegie provides timeless advice on effective communication, building relationships, and influencing others positively.

10. **David J. Schwartz**

   • **Books:** *The Magic of Thinking Big*

   • Schwartz encourages thinking beyond conventional limits to achieve personal and professional success.

11. **Maxwell Maltz**

   • **Books:** *Psycho-cybernetics*

   • Maltz explores the connection between self-image, success, and creativity.

12. **Claude M. Bristol**

   • **Books:** *The Magic of Believing*

   • Bristol explores the power of belief and how it can shape one's destiny.

13. **Peter B. Kyne**

   • **Books:** *The Go-Getter*

   • Kyne's book imparts valuable lessons on determination and achieving goals.

14. **RHJ**

   • **Books:** *It Works: The Little Red Book*

   • A concise guide to the power of positive thinking and manifestation.

15. **Russell H. Conwell**

   • **Books:** *Acres of Diamonds*

   • Conwell's book emphasises finding opportunities in one's own environment and recognizing the value of what is already at hand.

16. **James Allen**

   • **Books:** *As a Man Thinketh*

   • Allen's classic explores the impact of thoughts on character and circumstances, emphasising personal responsibility.

17. **Zig Ziglar**

   • **Books:** *See You At The Top*

   • Ziglar's teachings focus on motivation, goal-setting, and achieving success with a positive mindset.

18. **David Sereda**

   • **Private Membership Group:** *The Inner Circle*

   • David Sereda offers a community, products, and programs for those seeking personal and spiritual growth.

19. **Shahiroz Walji**

   • **Metaphysical Hub**

   • Shahiroz Walji's Metaphysical Hub provides resources and community for exploring metaphysical concepts.

20. **Proctor Gallagher Institute**

   • The Proctor Gallagher Institute focuses on personal development, prosperity, and transforming paradigms for success.

21. **Marisa Peer**

   • Marisa Peer is a renowned hypnotherapist and speaker, offering insights into transformation and mental well-being. Particularly known for her work in overcoming feelings of not being enough.

22. **Paul McKenna**

   • Paul McKenna provides resources for personal development and self-improvement through hypnosis and neuro-linguistic programming.

Consciousness, Quantum Physics, and Epigenetics:

1. **David R. Hawkins**

   • **Books:** *Map of Consciousness, Power Vs. Force* (and other books)

   • Hawkins explores the levels of human consciousness with a map to understand spiritual growth.

2. **Bruce H. Lipton, Ph.D.**

   • **Books:** *The Biology Of Belief, The Honeymoon Effect, Spontaneous Evolution*

   • Lipton's work bridges biology and spirituality, exploring how beliefs shape biology and influence health (epigenetics).

3. **Jacob Liberman**

   • **Books:** *Take Off Your Glasses and See: A Mind/Body Approach to Expanding Your Eyesight and Insight, Light: Medicine of the Future* (and other books)

   • Liberman combines a mind/body approach to vision, linking eyesight to broader insights and consciousness.

4. **Dr. Valerie V. Hunt**

   • **Books + DVDs:** *Infinite Mind: Science of the Human Vibrations of Consciousness, Uncork Your Consciousness* (and other books and DVDs)

   • Dr. Hunt delves into the science of human vibrations and their connection to consciousness.

5. **Dr. Konstantin Korotkov**

   • **Books:** *The Energy of Consciousness, Light After Life: Experiments and Ideas on After-Death Changes of Kirlian Pictures* (and other books)

   • Korotkov explores the scientific aspects of human energy fields and their relationship to consciousness.

6. **Dr. Joe Dispenza**

   • **Books:** *Becoming Supernatural, Breaking the Habit of Being Yourself* (and other books)

   • Dr. Joe Dispenza's work (books, courses, retreats) explores epigenetics.

7. **Gary Zukav**

   • **Books:** *Dancing Wu Li Masters: An Overview of the New Physics, The Seat of the Soul* (and other books)

   • Zukav explores the new physics, bridging science and spirituality.

8. **Fritjof Capra**

   • **Books:** *The Tao of Physics, The Turning Point* (and other books)

   • Capra explores parallels between modern physics and Eastern mysticism, highlighting the interconnectedness of science and spirituality.

ESP, Remote Viewing, Quantum Physics, and Consciousness Expansion:

1. Paul H. Smith

- **Book:** *The Essential Guide to Remote Viewing*
- Former CIA remote viewing trainer; offers programs in remote viewing and related skills. Smith is the longest serving Controlled Remote Viewing teacher from the US Army's Star Gate program.

2. Russell Targ

- **Books:** *Do You See What I See, The Reality of ESP* (and other books)
- Remote viewing and ESP. Targ is a physicist and researcher in remote viewing and extrasensory perception (ESP).

3. Ingo Swann

- **Books:** *Natural ESP, Preserving the Natural Child, Psychic Sexuality* (and other books)
- A researcher of the exceptional powers of the human mind and a leading figure in governmental and scientific projects to investigate and identify the scope of subtle human perceptions.

4. Dr. Dean Radin

- **Books:** *Real Magic, The Conscious Universe* (and other books)
- Explores psychic phenomena from a scientific lens.

5. ICU Academy

- ICU Academy provides training in remote viewing and psychic abilities.

6. Mark Komissarov and Mihaela Istrati

- Teaches InfoVision, a method for developing and utilising extrasensory perception.

7. The Monroe Institute

- The Monroe Institute provides programs focused on consciousness exploration through cutting-edge audio technology and immersive retreats.

8. **The Institute of Noetic Sciences**

    • Using science to explain phenomena not previously understood and harness the best of the mind to enhance human experience.

9. **The Parapsychological Association**

    • A professional organisation of scientists and scholars engaged in the study of 'psi' (or 'psychic') experiences, such as telepathy, clairvoyance, remote viewing, psychokinesis, psychic healing, and precognition.

10. **Dr. Fritz-Albert Popp**

    • Dr. Popp's research focuses on biophysics, particularly in biophotonics.

11. **Dan Winter**

    • Winter researches the physics of mystical experiences, gravitational energy, emotions, the evolution of consciousness, sacred geometry, quantum physics, and biofeedback.

12. **Dr. Fred Alan Wolf**

    • Wolf, a physicist and author, extensively explores the connections between quantum physics and consciousness.

13. **Dr. John Hagelin**

    • Hagelin's a quantum physicist whose research focuses on the role of consciousness in the universe and the potential of meditation to influence physical reality.

14. **Bruce Lipton**

    • **Books:** *The Biology of Belief, The Honeymoon Effect, Spontaneous Evolution*

    • Lipton, a cellular biologist and author, explores the connections between consciousness and biology, particularly in the science of epigenetics.

15. **Gregg Braden**

    • **Books:** *The God Code, The Divine Matrix, The Spontaneous Healing of Belief* (and other books)

    • Braden, a scientist and author, explores the science of consciousness and the impact of human emotion on physical reality.

Soul Matters, Past Lives, Dreams, Reincarnation, and Near Death Experiences:

1. Harold Klemp

- **Books:** *The Art of Spiritual Dreaming, ECK Wisdom on Karma and Reincarnation, Past Lives, Dreams, and Soul Travel* (and other books)
- Eckankar teaches techniques to explore one's inner worlds, including past lives, dreams, and Soul Travel.

2. Dr. Michael Newton

- **Book:** *Journey of Souls* (and other books)
- Explores the experiences of souls between lives. Through deep hypnosis sessions, Dr. Newton discovered that individuals could recall their existence as eternal spirits and describe their activities in the spirit world.

3. Dannion Brinkley

- **Books:** *10 Things to Know Before You Go, Saved by the Light* (and other books)
- Brinkley shares insights gained from his near-death experiences, providing wisdom on life and the afterlife.

4. Brian L. Weiss

- **Books:** *Through Time Into Healing, Same Soul, Many Bodies* (and other books)
- Weiss explores past lives and healing through regression therapy, emphasising the impact of past experiences on the present.

5. Raymond A. Moody Jr.

- **Books:** *The Light Beyond, Life After Life: The Investigation of a Phenomenon - Survival of Bodily Death* (and other books)
- Moody explores near-death experiences, shedding light on the transformative and spiritual aspects of these encounters.

6. NDE Stories

- A web compendium of near death experiences and resources from around the world. www.nderf.org

1. **Marguerite Mary Rigoglioso**

   • **Books:** *The Mystery Tradition of Miraculous Conception* (and other books)

   • Rigoglios's courses and books explore the concept of miraculous conception, particularly in the context of the divine feminine lineage.

2. **Sri Sai Kaleshwara Swami**

   • **Books:** *The Holy Womb; The Secrets of the Divine Mother's Creation* (and other books)

   • Sri Sai Kaleshwara Swami dives into the sacredness of the feminine.

3. **Den Poitras**

   • **Book: Parthenogenesis:** *Women's Long-Lost Ability to Self-Conceive*

   • Poitras explores the concept of parthenogenesis, the ability to self-conceive.

4. **Jessie E. Ayani**

   • **Books:** *The Lineage of the Codes of Light, The Priestess and Magus Trilogy* (and other books)

   • Ayani explores the codes of light within the feminine lineage, emphasising spiritual and transformative aspects, to awaken the gifts within ourselves.

5. **Maureen Walton**

   • **Book:** *The Good Darkness*

   • Walton's work reveals a hidden female creation technology called the "Blood Masteries" that activate a woman's magnetic toroidal systems. This can help a woman elevate to a superconscious level.

6. **Kaia Ra**

   • **Book:** *The Sophia Code*

   • Ra's book and programs are a divine feminine, modern sacred text. It is considered a living transmission that aims to activate spiritual evolution and awakening, reminding us of how precious we are.

7. **Margaret Starbird**

   • **Book:** *The Woman with the Alabaster Jar*

   • Starbird explores the figure of Mary Magdalene and the symbolism of the
   Holy Grail in relation to the divine feminine.

8. **Tom Kenyon and Judi Sion**

   • **Book:** *Magdalen Manuscript*

   • Kenyon and Sion delve into the alchemies of Horus and the sex magic
   of Isis, exploring sacred feminine mysteries.

9. **Elizabeth Seraphine**

   • **Program:** *The Priestess Path Lineages of Light Mystery School*

   • Seraphine offers resources and teachings on the priestess path and the divine
   feminine, supporting women to embody their priestess mantle and express their
   true power.

10. **The Lemurian Sisterhood and Shamanic Teaching Wheel**

   • **Program:** The Lemurian Sisterhood and Shamanic Teaching Wheel explores
   concepts related to the divine feminine.

11. **Seven Sisters Mystery School**

   • The Seven Sisters Mystery School offers teachings and practices related to
   the mysteries of the divine feminine that help restore the ancient way of the
   Priestess.

12. **Alison A. Armstrong**

   • **Books:** *The Queen's Code* (and other books)

   • Armstrong's books and programs explore the biological reasons behind the
   behaviour of women and help decode them.

13. **RC Blakes Jr.**

   • **Books:** *Queenology*, (and other books)

   • **Website:** Offers insights for reigning as a queen in spite of the odds, for
   reclaiming self-esteem, and having the courage to step into your true power.

The Alpha Male and Divine Masculine:

1. Alison A. Armstrong

- **Books:** *The Amazing Development of Men* (and other books)

- Armstrong's books and programs explore the journey of men from knights to princes to kings, providing insights into male development.

2. RC Blakes Jr.

- **Books:** *Kingology: The Return of the King* (and other books)

- RC Blakes Jr. delves into Kingology, guiding men on the path of returning to their true kingly nature.

3. Robert Moore and Douglas Gillette

- **Books:** *King, Warrior, Magician, Lover* (and other books)

- Moore and Gillette explore the archetypes of the mature masculine, emphasising psychological development.

4. Robert Bly

- **Book:** *Iron John: A Book About Men*

- Bly delves into the mythopoetic men's movement, exploring the journey to mature masculinity.

5. Brett and Kate McKay

- **Book:** *The Art of Manliness*

- The McKay's book and magazine offer classic skills and manners for the modern man, emphasising the traditional masculine virtues of a gentleman.

6. David Deida

- **Book:** *The Way of the Superior Man*

- Deida's book and program addresses the complexities of sexual and spiritual evolution in today's fast-paced world.

7. Men Without Masks

- Men Without Masks is a program for men to explore authentic masculinity through various resources and community.

Communication Styles of Men and Women:

1. **Alison A. Armstrong**

- **Books:** *The Queen's Code, Making Sense of Men* (and other books)

- Armstrong explores the reasons behind the behaviour of men and women, and fundamental differences in how we think, act, and communicate.

2. **RC Blakes Jr.**

- **Books:** *The Father-Daughter Talk* (and other books)

- Blakes guides men and women to embrace their inherent value and power.

3. **Gary Chapman**

- **Book:** *The 5 Love Languages*

- Chapman's book identifies different love languages, helping individuals understand and communicate love more effectively.

4. **John Gray**

- **Books:** *What Your Mother Couldn't Tell You and Your Father Didn't Know, Men are From Mars and Women are From Venus* (and other books)

- Gray's books and courses offer advanced relationship skills providing practical guidance for improving communication, and understanding the differences between men and women.

5. **Esther Perel**

- **Books:** *Mating in Captivity*

- Perel's work explores the complexities of maintaining intimacy in long-term relationships and the role of communication in erotic intelligence.

6. **Bibi Brzozka**

- Brzozka focuses on female orgasmic potential and fostering deeper intimacy through effective communication.

7. **Jaiya**

- Jaiya's Erotic Blueprints provide a framework for empowered sexual communication, erotic ecstasy, and enhanced understanding between partners.

Taoism and Inner Alchemy:

1. **Lao-Tzu**

- **Book:** *Tao Te Ching*

- A classical Chinese text and foundational work of Taoism written around 400 BC and credited to the sage Laozi. In eighty-one chapters, Lao-tzu's Tao Te Ching, or Book of the Way, provides imparts advice on balance and perspective, a serene and generous spirit, and how to work for the good with the effortless skill that comes from being in accord with the Tao—the basic principle of the universe.

2. **Daniel Reid**

- **Book:** *The Tao of Health, Sex & Longevity* (and other books)

- Reid explores Taoist principles related to health, sex, and longevity, including the connection between inner alchemy and well-being.

3. **Dr. Stephen Chang**

- **Books:** *The Tao of Sexology, The Great Tao* (and other books)

- Chang's work delves into the Taoist perspective on sexology, using sexual techniques to enhance health, and Taoism; emphasising inner alchemy and its transformative effects on body and mind.

4. **Dr. Felice Dunas**

- **Book:** *Passion Play* (and other books)

- Dunas's books and courses incorporate powerful Taoist principles to improve health, sex, and intimacy, rectifying sexual dissatisfaction.

5. **Mantak & Maneewan Chia**

- **Books:** *Healing Love through the Tao: Cultivating Male Sexual Energy, The Multi-Orgasmic Couple* (and other books)

- The Chia's books and courses focus on cultivating male and female sexual energy, sexual secrets for couples, and enhanced intimacy through Taoist practices. These include learning to separate orgasm and ejaculation and retention practices for longevity and vitality, leading to multiple orgasm potential.

6. **Mantak Chia and Douglas Abrams**

   • **Book:** *The Multi-Orgasmic Man*

   • This collaborative work provides insights into sexual secrets every man should know, rooted in Taoist principles. These include learning to separate orgasm and ejaculation and retention practices for longevity and vitality, leading to multiple orgasm potential.

7. **Bruce Frantzis**

   • **Book:** *Taoist Sexual Meditation* (and other books)

   • Frantzis explores the connection between love, energy, and spirit through Taoist sexual meditation, emphasising communication within intimate relationships.

8. **Richard Wilhelm**

   • **Book:** *The Secret of the Golden Flower: A Chinese Book of Life*

   • The translation of this classic work explores the teachings of Taoism, including inner alchemy and the transformative journey of life. The language is flowery and sounds poetic, yet within lie many pearls of wisdom.

9. **Hsi Lai**

   • **Book:** *The Sexual Teachings of the White Tigress: Secrets of the Female Taoist Masters* (and other books)

   • Lai delves into the teachings of female Taoist masters within the context of sexual and spiritual wisdom.

10. **Thomas Cleary**

   • **Book:** *The Taoist Classics, Volume 1* (and other books)

   • Cleary's translations provide access to essential Taoist texts, offering insights into inner alchemy and Taoist philosophy.

11. **John Heider**

   • **Books:** *The Tao of Leadership, The Tao of Daily Living*

   • Heider applies Taoist principles to leadership, emphasising effective communication and harmony in relationships.

12. **Eva Wong**

   • **Books:** Taoism: *An Essential Guide, Cultivating Stillness: A Taoist Manual for Transforming Body and Mind* (and other books)

   • Wong's books provide an overview of Taoism, including its principles of inner alchemy and communication.

13. **Robert Lawlor**

   • **Book:** *Earth Honoring: The New Male Sexuality* (and other books)

   • Lawlor explores sexual behaviour in ancient traditions like Tantra and Taoism, offering insights into redirecting male energy from excess to constructive paths. He details specific techniques used in sexual and spiritual training to harness creative potential and spiritual growth.

Martial Arts Philosophy:

1. **Patrick McCarthy**

   • **Book:** *The Bubishi*

   • Treasured for centuries by top martial arts masters, the Bubishi is a classic Chinese work on philosophy, strategy, medicine, and technique as they relate to the martial arts. For hundreds of years, the Bubishi was a secret text passed from master to student in China and later in Okinawa. No other classic work has had as dramatic an impact on the shaping and development of karate as the Bubishi. Karate historian and authority Patrick McCarthy spent over ten years researching and studying the Bubishi and the arts associated with it. His work includes groundbreaking research on Okinawan and Chinese history, as well as the fighting and healing traditions that developed in those countries, making it a gold mine for researchers and practitioners alike.

2. **Richard Kim**

   • **Book:** *The Classical Man* (and other books)

   • Kim's work explores martial arts philosophy, emphasising character development. This book shares the historically significant lives of real martial arts masters.

3. **Deng Ming-Dao**

   • **Book:** *Chronicles of the Tao: The Secret Life of a Taoist Master* (and other books)

• Ming-Dao's chronicles provide insights into the real life and wisdom of Taoist master, Kwan Saihung who was born into a wealthy martial arts family and became the thirteenth and last discipline of the grand master of the sacred mountain known as Huashan.

4. Chen Kaiguo, Zheng Shunchao, Thomas Cleary

• **Book:** *Opening the Dragon Gate: The Making of a Modern Taoist Wizard*

• The biography of Wang Liping, a modern Taoist wizard, is the true story of how a young boy becomes heir to a tradition of esoteric knowledge and practice through an arduous fifteen-year apprenticeship, learning the true source of health, healing, and long life.

5. Soke C. J. Rupert Juta

• **Book:** *Tao-Shukokairyu Odyssey* (and other books)

• Juta's work explores the martial arts style and philosophy of Tao-Shukokairyu, offering insights into the journey of a martial artist, focusing on mindset and critical thinking.

6. Gichin Funakoshi

• **Book:** *Karate-Do: My Way of Life*

• Funakoshi, known as the "Father of Karate-do," shares his journey from the secrecy of Okinawan self-defence to the global practice of martial arts. Funakoshi refined techniques and emphasised spirituality. Through anecdotes of his renowned teachers and personal trials, he unveils the essence of authentic karate and exemplifies principles of perseverance, self-reliance, and samurai ethos.

7. Bruce Lee

• **Book:** *The Tao of Jeet Kune Do*

• The book details the science and philosophy behind the fighting system Lee pioneered. It is the original mixed martial art known as Jeet Kune Do—"the way of the intercepting fist.

8. Miyamoto Musashi

• **Book:** *The Book of Five Rings*

• Musashi's classic work presents martial arts philosophy through the lens of strategy and the way of the samurai.

9. **Joe Hyams**

  • **Book:** *Zen in the Martial Arts*

  • Hyams reveals how the daily application of Zen principles developed his physical expertise and gave him the mental discipline to control his personal problems, and how understanding the spiritual goals in martial arts can dramatically alter the quality of your life.

10. **Forrest E. Morgan**

  • **Book:** *Living the Martial Way*

  • Morgan's book offers a step-by-step approach to applying the Japanese warrior's mindset to martial training and daily life.

11. **Sun Tzu**

  • **Book:** *The Art of War*

  • An ancient Chinese military treatise composed of 13 chapters and attributed to the military strategist Sun Tzu. It explores skills dedicated to warfare and how it applies to military strategy and tactics including psychology.

Shamanism and Psychedelic Plants:

1. **Mircea Eliade**

  • **Book:** *Shamanism: Archaic Techniques of Ecstasy* (and other books)

  • Eliade surveys the tradition of shamanism (at once magicians and medicine men and women, healers and miracle-doers, priests, mystics, and poets) through two and a half millennia of human history, illuminating the magico-religious life of societies.

2. **Michael Harner**

  • **Book:** *The Way of the Shaman* (and other books)

  • Harner's book introduces core shamanic practices and principles, shedding light on the role of shamans in different societies, what it is, where it came from, and how you can participate.

3. **Lynn Andrews**

  • **Book:** *The Medicine Woman book series* (and other books)

  • Andrews' books, programs, and mystery school offer training into modern-day shamanism and the divine feminine, offering insights into healing and wisdom.

4. **Andrew Weil**

   • **Books:** *The Natural Mind, The Marriage of the Sun and Moon* (and other books)

   • In The Natural Mind, Weil suggests that the desire to alter consciousness periodically is an innate, normal human drive. In The Marriage of the Sun and the Moon, he examines the integration of masculine and feminine energies, drawing inspiration from shamanic experiences.

5. **Carlos Castaneda**

   • **Book:** *The Teachings of Don Juan: A Yaqui Way of Knowledge*
   (and other books)

   • Castaneda's books recount Don Juan's apprenticeship with a Yaqui Indian shaman, exploring shamanic teachings and a new way of seeing the world.

6. **Eliot Cowan**

   • **Book:** *Plant Spirit Medicine*

   • Cowan's book explores the healing potential of plant spirits, connecting shamanic principles with the medicinal properties of plants.

7. **Jeremy Narby**

   • **Book:** *The Cosmic Serpent: DNA and the Origins of Knowledge*

   • Narby investigates the connection between shamanic knowledge and DNA, exploring the mysteries of consciousness and evolution.

Health (Wholeness) and Healing:

1. **Dr. Bradley Nelson**

   • **Books:** *The Emotion Code, The Body Code*

   • Nelson's books and work focuses on techniques that release trapped emotions to ease physical and emotional ailments.

2. **Dr. Ryke Geerd Hamer**

   • **Book:** *Summary of the New Medicine*

   • Hamer's work presents a very different approach to understanding cancer, how diseases develop, and the mind-body connection. His research led him to believe that diseases are a result of biological conflict, shock, or trauma (if not a result of poison or an injury). He discovered that each biological conflict leaves a visible mark in the brain (confirmed by a CT scan) and that the nature of the conflict predetermined the site of the disease. The result of his research was the creation of a disease chart that accurately describes the biological conflict cause of each disease, the exact location in the brain where the focus is found, and how the disease manifests during the conflict active phase and resolution phases.

3. David R. Hawkins

* **Books:** *The Spectrum of Consciousness Explained: A Proven Energy Scale to Actualize Your Ultimate Potential, Power Vs. Force, Healing and Recovery* (and other books)

* Hawkins' work explores healing and recovery from a spiritual perspective, integrating consciousness and health. He developed a map that defines a range of values, attitudes, and emotions that correspond to levels of consciousness and provides practical applications to help people heal and evolve to higher levels of consciousness and energy. He posits that an individual's power and level of consciousness can be enhanced through greater integrity, understanding, and compassion.

4. Lars Muhl

* **Book:** *The Gate of Light: Healing Practices to Connect You to Source Energy* (and other books)

* Muhl's book is an introduction to the long-forgotten healing methods of the Essenes, and offers useful tools, meditations, and visualisations for modern-day practitioners.

5. Deepak Chopra

* **Book:** *Quantum Healing: Exploring the Frontiers of Mind/Body Medicine* (and other books)

* Chopra's work combines Western medicine, neuroscience, and physics with the insights of Ayurvedic theory to show that the human body is controlled by a "network of intelligence" grounded in quantum reality. Not a superficial psychological state, this intelligence lies deep enough to change the basic patterns that design our physiology, with the potential to overcome illness.

6. Michael Breus

* **Book:** *The Power of When*

* Breus's work on the science of sleep presents a groundbreaking program for

getting back in sync with your natural rhythm (chronobiology) by making minor changes to your daily routine. Working with your body's inner clock for maximum health, happiness, and productivity becomes easy and fun.

7. Felice Dunas

- **Book:** *Passion Play* (and other books)

- Dunas's books and courses focus on healing through pleasure; incorporating powerful Taoist principles to improve health, sex, and intimacy, leading to more meaningful connections and a more satisfying life.

8. Nadia Volf

- **Book:** *Mysteries of the Ear: Secrets of Well-Being*

- Volf is the creator of the Auricular Causative Diagnostic method. Her work reveals the extraordinary powers of the auricular (ear) acupuncture points, making it possible to provide relief for everyday ailments.

9. Konstantin Sukhov

- **Book:** *Clinical Hirudotherapy: Practical Guide: Book 1. General Hirudotherapy* (and other books)

- Sukhov's guide explores the therapeutic use of medicinal leeches, known as hirudotherapy, to address a wide array of health complaints.

10. HP Ekkehard Scheller

- **Book:** *Candidalism*

- Scheller's work examines the impact of candida overgrowth on health and well-being, contributing to the understanding of candidalism. Borrelias, viruses, and other pathogens have learned to camouflage themselves to keep from being attacked by our immune system and strong drugs. Thanks to Dark Field Microscopy of blood and Radionic Testing, Ekkehard Sirian Scheller discovered the camouflaged Candida fungi, which varied their shape to keep from being detected. Due to the fermentation of glucose, extreme mycotoxins are produced, which destroy the mucosal system due to constant corrosion. As a result, many secondary diseases arise.

11. Artour Rakhimov

- **Book:** *Breathing Slower and Less: The Greatest Health Discovery Ever* (Buteyko Method) (and other books)

• Rakhimov's book explores the health benefits of the buteyko breathing method and its impact on well-being. Learn how breathing retraining can prevent and alleviate many diseases, along with insights from clinical trials, lifestyle factors, and breathing retraining techniques. Embark on a journey to long-term health and vitality.

12. James Nestor

• **Book: Breath:** *The New Science of a Lost Art*

• Nestor's exploration of breath delves into the science and art of breathing, emphasising its crucial role in health.

13. Ben Greenfield

• **Book:** *Boundless: Upgrade Your Brain, Optimize Your Body, & Defy Aging*

• Greenfield is a walking encyclopedia of biohacking wisdom, blending cutting-edge science with practical tips for a vibrant life. As a health consultant, speaker, and author, he aims to optimise life for boundless energy and fulfilment through his books, podcasts and coaching. He specialises in longevity, anti-aging, biohacking, and positive psychology.

14. Dr. Gabor Maté

• **Book:** *When the Body Says No: The Cost of Hidden Stress, The Myth of Normal: Trauma, Illness, and Healing in a Toxic Culture* (and other books)

• An addiction expert, Dr. Maté is the creator of the psychotherapeutic approach, Compassionate Inquiry. His books and work explore the connection between stress, emotions, and addiction and disease, offering insights into the mind-body connection.

15. Bessel van der Kolk

• **Book:** *The Body Keeps the Score: Brain, Mind, and Body in the Healing of Trauma*

• Van der Kolk's influential work explores the impact of trauma on the body and mind, offering approaches to healing.

16. Dr. Anna Lembke

• **Book:** *Dopamine Nation: Finding Balance in the Age of Indulgence*

• Lembke's book explores the role of dopamine in modern society and its impact on health, addiction, and well-being.

17. **Jonathon Aslay**

   • **Book:** *What The Heck Is Self-Love Anyway?*

   • Aslay's book and relationship coaching focus on self-love as a fundamental aspect of health and well-being, contributing to personal development and healthy relationships.

18. **Barbara Ann Brennan**

   • **Book:** *Hands of Light: A Guide to Healing Through the Human Energy Field* (and other books)

   • Brennan's book explores energy healing through the human energy field, offering insights into holistic health practices.

19. **Emily Matweow**

   • Emily Matweow is a master energy healer and medical intuitive specialising in energy healing, medical intuition, removing blocks, and empowering clients to regain balance, clarity, and peace.

20. **Alvin De Leon**

   • Dr. Alvin De Leon focuses on empowered health through the principles of Dr. Hamer's German New Medicine, based on the 5 biological laws.

21. **Brent Bruning**

   • **Book:** *The Power in Your Hands*

   • Bruning's work specialises in breaking through trauma patterns using biological blueprints as seen in the hands, offering innovative approaches to healing. Web: www.thepowerinyourhands.com

   • **Bonus for readers! Coupon Codes for:**
      • A 2-hour Hand Analysis + Life Pattern Session
      Coupon code: StoryMaster (receive $100 off)
      • The Shift or The Hero's Journey program: Mastering your shadows to break through to your exalted Self
      Coupon code: StorymasterProduct (receive $100 off)

22. **David Sereda**

   • David Sereda offers frequency-based healing products and programs, exploring the intersection of sound, vibrational alignment, and health.

23. **Medical Medium Anthony William**

    • **Books:** *Brain Saver, Thyroid Healing, Medical Medium* (and other books)

    • Medical Medium Anthony William was born with the unique ability to converse with the Spirit of Compassion, who provides him with extraordinarily advanced healing information far ahead of its time. He is considered a chronic illness expert and is the originator of the global celery juice movement and Brain Shot Therapy.

24. **Vibrational Revelations with Elena Bensenoff and Alejandro Ferradas**

    • Using integrative and quantum medicine, paired with vibrational frequency measurements of your level of consciousness (based on the work of David R. Hawkins's map of consciousness), Elena Bensenoff and Alejandro Ferradas offer resources on vibrational healing and frequency readings for clients.

25. **Bio-resonance Life Flow: Health Scans & Consultations with Yvette Farkas**

    • Get a clear picture of your health with a bio-resonance scan. It tests for viruses, bacteria, mold, parasites, allergies, food intolerances, heavy metals, inflammation, and more. Even the strength of the auric field is shown. Detailed health scans provide insights into energetic imbalances and blocks to health, empowering you to make more informed decisions to increase vitality, wellbeing, and energy. Web: www.bioresonancescans.com

26. **Thich Nhat Hanh: International Plum Village Community**

    • Thich Nhat Hanh is a Zen master, the founder of Plum Village, numerous movements and charities, and the author of over 100 books focusing on mindfulness.

27. **HeartMath Institute**

    • The HeartMath Institute explores the connection between heart health, emotions, and overall well-being, offering practical tools for self-regulation.

28. **Bryan Johnson**

    • Bryan Johnson's biohacking protocol focuses on health optimization, contributing to personalised approaches to wellbeing.

29. **Edgar Cayce's Association for Research and Enlightenment (A.R.E.)**

    • **Book:** *The Essential Edgar Cayce* (and other books)

• The Association for Research and Enlightenment (A.R.E.) offers body-mind-spirit resources and educational programs that foster personal transformation through the wisdom embedded in the extensive collection of Edgar Cayce's readings. Edgar Cayce is a twentieth-century seer and intuitive healer. The book features Cayce's most intriguing and influential readings, and a biographical introduction to his life.

30. Diagnostic Testing of One's Biological Age

• TruDiagnostic offers diagnostic testing of one's biological age, providing insights into overall health and longevity.

Yoga Philosophy:

1. Swami Sivananda

• **Books:** *Bliss Divine, Practice of Bhakti Yoga* (and other books)

• Swami Sivananda is the founder of the The Divine Life Society, the inspiration behind the Sivananda Yoga Vedanta Centres and Yasodhara ashrams, and the author of over 300 books.

2. Swami Sivananda Radha

• **Books:** *Mantras; Words of Power, Radha; Diary of a Woman's Search* (and other books)

• Swami Sivananda Radha is the founder of Canada's first ashram - Yasodhara Ashram, and opened the Yoga Vedanta bookstore.

3. Swami Vishnu-Devananda

• **Books:** *Meditation and Mantras, The Classical Illustrated Book of Yoga* (and other books)

• Swami Vishnu-Devananda founded the Sivananda Yoga Vedanta Centres and is the author of numerous books.

4. Swami Satchidananda

• **Books:** *The Yoga Sutras of Patanjali, Key to Peace* (and other books)

• Swami Satchidananda founded Integral Yoga International and Satchidananda Ashram - Yogaville and is the author of numerous books.

5. **Swami Satyananda**

- **Books:** *Asana, Pranayama, Mudra, and Bandha, Yoga Nidra* (and other books)

- Swami Satyananda founded International Yoga Fellowship Movement and The Bihar School of Yoga, and authored numerous books.

6. **The Bhagavad Gita**

- The Bhagavad Gita (Sanskrit: "Song of God") is a foundational text in yoga philosophy, offering profound teachings on duty, righteousness, and the path to spiritual realisation.

7. **Sri Kaleshwar**

- **Book:** *The Holy Womb - The Secrets of The Divine Mother's Creation: A Rendering of the Teachings of Sri Sai Kaleshwara Swami* (and other books)

- Kaleshwar's work delves into the mysteries of divine consciousness, contributing to the understanding of spirituality and self-realisation.

8. **Yogacharya B.K.S.Iyengar**

- **Book:** *Light on Yoga: The Bible of Modern Yoga* (and other books)

- B.K.S.Iyengar founded the Ramamani Iyengar Memorial Yoga Institute (RIMYI) and authored numerous books.

9. **TKV Desikachar**

- **Book:** *The Heart of Yoga: Developing a Personal Practice* (and other books)

- TKV Desikachar developed Viniyoga and founded the Krishnamacharya Yoga Mandiram (KYM), and has authored numerous books.

10. **Sri Aurobindo + The Mother**

- Sri Aurobindo is the author of several books and co-founder with The Mother of the Sri Aurobindo Ashram. In addition to spending 50 years overseeing the growth of this many-faceted spiritual community, The Mother established Sri Aurobindo International Centre of Education, and an international township called Auroville.

Ayurveda (The Science of Life):

1. Dr. Robert E. Svoboda

- **Books:** *Ayurveda: Life, Health and Longevity, Prakriti: Your Ayurvedic Constitution* (and other books)

- Dr. Robert Svoboda's books and programs provide a comprehensive overview of Ayurveda, exploring its principles and practices for maintaining health and longevity.

2. Dr. Vasant Dattatray Lad

- **Books:** *Ayurveda: The Science of Self-Healing: A Practical Guide, The Complete Book of Ayurvedic Home Remedies* (and other books)

- Dr. Vasant Lad is the founder of the Ayurvedic Institute and the author of 12 books. His work disseminates the timeless principles and practices of Ayurvedic - The Science of Life.

3. Dr. David Frawley and Dr. Vasant Dattatray Lad

- **Book:** *The Yoga of Herbs: An Ayurvedic Guide to Herbal Medicine*

- This collaborative work explores the intersection of Ayurveda and herbal medicine, offering insights into natural healing.

4. Dr. David Frawley

- **Book:** *Ayurveda and the Mind: The Healing of Consciousness* (and other books)

- Dr. David Frawley is the founder of The American Institute of Vedic Studies and author of several books exploring the rich knowledge of Ayurveda.

5. Maya Bri. Tiwari

- **Book:** *Ayurveda: Secrets of Healing* (and other books)

- Maya Tiwari is the founder of The Wise Earth School of Ayurveda and Mother Om Mission (MOM). Her books and work share the healing path of Ayurveda, unveiling its secrets for healing and maintaining balance.

6. Amadea Morningstar

- **Book:** *The Ayurvedic Cookbook* (and other books)

- Amadea Morningstar is the founder of the Ayurveda Polarity Therapy and Yoga Institute. She is an author, speaker, and Ayurvedic practitioner and instructor.

Sacred Geometry and Physics:

1. Gyorgy Doczi

- **Book:** *The Power of Limits: Proportional Harmonies in Nature, Art, and Architecture*
- Doczi explores the concept of proportional harmonies in various aspects of life, art, and architecture through sacred geometry.

2. Robert Lawlor

- **Book:** *Sacred Geometry: Philosophy and Practice* (and other books)
- Lawlor's work delves into the philosophical and practical aspects of sacred geometry, exploring its significance in diverse disciplines.

3. Matila Ghyka

- **Book:** *The Geometry of Art and Life*
- Ghyka's book connects geometry with art and life, revealing the inherent mathematical principles that underlie both.

4. Les Brown

- **Book:** *The Pyramid*
- This resource explores the use of pyramids for healing and meditation, offering insights into their potential benefits.

5. NOAA - Magnetic Field Calculators

- The NOAA website provides tools for calculating the Earth's magnetic field, including declination, useful for aligning pyramids with the Earth's magnetic forces.

6. David Sereda

- Sereda, a researcher and filmmaker, offers insights into UFOs, quantum physics, and spirituality, providing a deeper understanding of the universe and human potential.

7. David Wilcock

- Wilcock, a researcher and lecturer, explores the convergence of science and spirituality, investigating topics like UFOs, consciousness, and the universe's mysteries, often incorporating sacred geometry and metaphysical concepts.

Finances and Wealth:

1. Ken Honda

> **Book:** *Happy Money: The Japanese Art of Making Peace with Your Money*
> (and other books)
> • Ken Honda explores the relationship between happiness and money, offering insights from Japanese philosophy to create a harmonious connection with finances.

2. T. Harv Eker

> **Book:** *Secrets of the Millionaire Mind: Mastering the Inner Game of Wealth*
> • Eker delves into the mindset and psychological aspects that contribute to financial success, providing guidance on cultivating a wealthy mindset.

3. Robert G. Allen

> **Book:** *Multiple Streams of Income: How to Generate a Lifetime of Unlimited Wealth!*
> • Allen introduces the concept of creating multiple income streams for long-term financial success, outlining strategies for generating wealth.

4. Sam Rossi and Andra Pickens

> **Book:** *Quantum Networking: How to Play the Game that the Wealthiest and Happiest People Play... Starting Today*
> • Rossi and Pickens explore the principles of quantum networking, offering a unique perspective on building connections for financial success.

5. George S. Clason

> **Book:** *The Richest Man in Babylon*
> • Clason's classic imparts timeless financial wisdom through parables set in ancient Babylon, addressing principles of wealth-building.

6. Thomas J. Stanley and William D. Danko

> **Book:** *The Millionaire Next Door: The Surprising Secrets of America's Wealthy*
> • Stanley and Danko reveal common traits and habits of self-made millionaires, challenging stereotypes and offering practical insights for building wealth.

7. **Napoleon Hill**

   • **Book:** *Think and Grow Rich*

   • Hill's seminal work outlines principles for success and wealth, emphasising the power of mindset and goal-setting.

8. **Morgan Housel**

   • **Book:** *The Psychology of Money: Timeless Lessons on Wealth, Greed, and Happiness*

   • Housel explores the psychological aspects of money management, providing insights into the behaviours that influence financial decisions.

9. **Alex Hormozi**

   • **Book:** *$100M Offers: How to Make Offers So Good People Feel Stupid Saying No*

   • Hormozi shares strategies for crafting irresistible offers that create compelling opportunities for financial success.

10. **Tony Robbins**

    • **Book:** *MONEY Master the Game: 7 Simple Steps to Financial Freedom*
    (and other books)

    • Robbins' work provides practical steps for achieving financial and personal freedom to live your best life.

11. **Robert & Kim Kiyosaki**

    • **Book:** *Rich Dad, Poor Dad: What the Rich Teach Their Kids About Money - That the Poor and Middle Class Do Not!* (and other books)

    • The Kiyosaki's books, programs and games offer educational programs for financial freedom that are simple enough for a 9-year old to understand.

12. **Bob Proctor**

    • **Book:** *You Were Born Rich*

    • Proctor's teachings focus on unlocking one's innate potential for wealth and success, emphasising the abundance within each individual.

13. **Ramit Sethi**

    • **Book:** *I Will Teach You to Be Rich*

    • Sethi's book and courses provide practical advice on personal finance, covering topics such as saving, investing, and creating a rich life.

Behaviour and Body Language:

1. Chris Voss

- **Book:** *Never Split the Difference: Negotiating As If Your Life Depended On It*

- Voss, a former FBI negotiator, shares negotiation techniques and strategies, providing insights into effective communication and persuasion.

2. Vanessa Van Edwards

- **Book: Captivate:** *The Science of Succeeding with People*

- Van Edwards explores the science of interpersonal communication, offering practical tips and strategies for connecting with others.

3. Joe Navarro

- **Book:** *What Every Body is Saying*

- Navarro, a former FBI agent, decodes nonverbal communication, providing insights into reading body language for improved understanding and communication.

4. Rebecca Zung

- **Book:** *How to Negotiate with a Bully (Narcissist)*

- Zung provides guidance on negotiating with challenging personalities, particularly narcissists, offering strategies for effective communication.

5. Ramani Durvasula, PhD

- **Book:** *It's Not You*

- Dr. Durvasula explores relationships with narcissists, providing insights into understanding and navigating these challenging dynamics.

Transmitted and Channelled Information:

1. Kryon

- **Books:** *Don't Think Like a Human, The Twelve Layers of DNA, The Indigo Children, The Women of Lemuria* (and other books)

- Kryon offers channelled information via books, programs, and retreats, providing spiritual insights and teachings, contributing to personal and collective transformation.

2. Abraham Hicks

- **Books:** *Ask and It is Given: Learning to Manifest Your Desires, The Astonishing Power of Emotions* (and other books)

- Abraham Hicks, channelled by Esther Hicks, shares teachings on the law of attraction, manifestation, and spiritual guidance via books, programs, and retreats.

3. Law of One

- The Law of One provides channelled material offering perspectives on spirituality, the nature of reality, and the evolution of consciousness.

4. Ashayana Deane

- **Books:** *Voyagers: The Sleeping Abductees - Volume 1, Voyagers: The Secrets of Amenti - Volume 2* (and other books)

- Ashayana Deane's work explores ascension mechanics and multidimensional consciousness, providing insights into spiritual evolution.

5. Sarah Landon

- **Books:** *The Wisdom of the Council: Channelled Messages for Living Your Purpose, The Dream, The Journey, Eternity, And God: Channeled Answers to Life's Deepest Questions*

- Sarah Landon shares channelled information and spiritual teachings to assist individuals on their path of self-discovery and personal growth.

6. Emily Matweow

- **Book:** *INTUITION: Discover 11 Different Kinds* (and other books)

- Emily Matweow is a master energy healer and medical intuitive, providing insights and guidance for holistic well-being.

7. Lee Harris

- **Book:** *Conversations with the Z's*

- Harris is an energy intuitive, author, and musician. His grounded, practical teachings focus on the expansion of awareness to help you live a more heart-centred life.

Conscious Leadership, Mentorship, and Coaching:

1. **MindValley**

- MindValley offers personal development and education programs, focusing on holistic growth, consciousness, and well-being.

2. **Regan Hillyer**

- Regan Hillyer provides coaching and mentorship for individuals seeking personal and financial transformation, emphasising conscious leadership.

3. **Juan Pa Barahona**

- Juan Pa Barahona offers coaching and mentorship, guiding individuals towards personal and professional success through conscious leadership.

4. **Marcel Szenessy**

- Marcel Szenessy provides seminars and coaching, emphasising personal development and conscious leadership for individuals and organisations.

5. **Yvette Farkas**

- Yvette Farkas is a health-based coach and mentor, an author, and practitioner of ancient healing practices taking people back to their health and their hearts.

6. **Daria Vodopianova**

- Daria Vodopianova contributes to conscious leadership and mentorship, focusing on empowering individuals in their personal and professional journeys.

7. **Tony Robbins**

- Tony Robbins is a renowned life coach and motivational speaker, offering programs and events focused on personal development, wealth creation, and leadership.

8. **Brent Bruning**

- Brent Bruning's work specialises in breaking through trauma patterns using biological blueprints as seen in the hands, offering innovative approaches to healing through in-depth coaching and mentorship.

Other:

1. **David Wilcock**

- **Book:** *Awakening in the Dream:Contact with the Divine* (and other books)

- Wilcock explores topics related to consciousness, spirituality, and the nature of reality, providing insights into awakening and self-discovery.

2. **Jessie Ayani**

- **Book:** *The Brotherhood of the Magi* (and other books)

- Ayani's work explores mystical and esoteric themes, offering insights into ancient wisdom and the spiritual journey of the Magi.

3. **Vladimir Nikolaevich Megre**

- **Book: Anastasia:** *Ringing Cedars of Russia* (9 books)

- Megre's "Anastasia" series revolves around a Siberian recluse named Anastasia, sharing her wisdom on nature, spirituality, and the interconnectedness of all life.

4. **Michael A. Singer**

- **Book:** *The Surrender Experiment: My Journey into Life's Perfection* (and other books)

- Singer recounts his personal journey of surrendering to life's flow, providing a profound exploration of spiritual surrender and personal growth.

5. **Zecharia Sitchin**

- **Book:** *The Anunnaki Chronicles: A Zecharia Sitchin Reader* (and other books)

- Sitchin's collection delves into ancient Sumerian texts, offering interpretations and insights into the possible extraterrestrial influence on human history.

6. **Peter Ragnar**

- **Book:** *Finding Heart: How to Live with Courage in a Confusing World*

- Ragnar shares his perspective on courage and navigating life's challenges, providing insights and practical wisdom for personal development.

7. **Richard P. Feynman**

- **Book:** *Surely You're Joking, Mr. Feynman! Adventures of a Curious Character*

• Feynman's memoir offers humorous anecdotes and reflections on his life as a physicist, showcasing his curious and playful approach to understanding the world.

8. Joseph Campbell

• **Book:** *The Power of Myth* (and other books)

• Campbell explores the power of myth and its role in human culture, drawing connections between ancient stories and contemporary life.

9. Dan Millman

• **Book:** *Way of the Peaceful Warrior*

• Millman's novel combines fiction and autobiographical elements, conveying spiritual teachings through the story of a young athlete's journey toward enlightenment.

10. Rudolf Steiner

• **Book:** *Bees*

• Steiner delves into the spiritual significance of bees and their role in the natural world, offering insights into the interconnectedness of life.

11. Jacqueline Freeman

• **Book:** *Song of Increase: Returning to Our Sacred Relationship with Honeybees*

• Freeman explores the sacred relationship between humans and honeybees, emphasising the spiritual and ecological importance of these creatures.

12. Richard Bach

• **Book:** *Illusions: The Adventures of a Reluctant Messiah* (and other books)

• Bach's philosophical novel explores the nature of reality, illusion, and the potential for each individual to discover their divine nature.

13. Hermann Hesse

• **Book:** *Siddhartha*

• Hesse's novel follows the journey of Siddhartha, exploring themes of self-discovery, enlightenment, and the spiritual path.

14. **Robin Sharma**

   • **Book:** *The Monk Who Sold His Ferrari*

   • Sharma's book combines fiction and self-help, telling the story of a successful lawyer's spiritual journey toward a more meaningful and fulfilling life.

15. **Neale Donald Walsch**

   • **Books:** *Conversations With God: An Uncommon Dialogue (Books 1-3)* (and other books)

   • Walsch's book presents a dialogue with the divine, offering profound insights into spirituality and the soul's journey.

Devices for Health and Healing:

1. **David Sereda's Products (the largest frequency library in the world)**

   • Sereda offers a diverse range of products, including frequency libraries, designed to promote health and well-being through vibrational and energy principles. Web: www.davidsereda.co

2. **Safe Laser**

   • A new generation of lasers for therapeutic use. The Safe Laser family has analgesic and anti-inflammatory effects and speeds up healing and regeneration of the body. Web: www.safelaser.hu/en

3. **Jonathan Goldman's Chakra Chants Tuning Forks**

   • Goldman's tuning forks are designed to align with chakras, offering a sound-based approach to balancing and harmonising energy centres in the body

4. **Bio-Well**

   • Bio-Well is a device that measures and visualises the human energy field, providing insights into overall wellbeing and energy balance.
   Web: www.bio-well.store

5. **SomaVedic**

   • Products that utilise frequency therapy and natural science to harmonise spaces and water, and reduce the impact of harmful EMFs.
   Web: www.somavedic.com

The Most Important Things I Learned From This Book: